Mine for Keeps

Mine for Keeps

by Jean Little

With illustrations by Lewis Parker

LITTLE, BROWN AND COMPANY
Boston *Toronto*

LIBRARY OF CONGRESS CATALOG CARD NO. 62–12381

EIGHTH PRINTING

Published simultaneously in Canada
by Little, Brown & Company (Canada) Limited

PRINTED IN THE UNITED STATES OF AMERICA

Contents

To Dad

Mine for Keeps

1

Wish Come True

SAL COPELAND was scared.

When she watched the cottony clouds brush under the wing of the plane or caught a glimpse of the earth far below, she forgot and felt all right for a moment. Then she would remember.

"I am going home to stay," she would say to herself—and the queer cold feeling would come back.

She had been living at the Allendale School for Handicapped Children for over five years. During those years she had often gone home. There had been two holidays every year, one at Christmas and one in the summer. Sal had always spent these with her family. But this time, going home was different. This time, nobody would be taking her back to school in three weeks. Right now—this very minute—Dad was bringing her home for good! The closer she got, the queerer she felt.

Sal could not understand it. Almost ever since she could remember, she had longed, more than anything, to live at home. Whenever she had seen a first star through a window at school, she had rhymed off "Star light, star bright . . ." as fast as she could—and every time, her wish was the same, *Let me live at home.* It had been her wish before blowing out her birthday candles for as far back as she could remember, and it was the last bit in her prayers every night.

So what could be wrong? Her wish was coming true. Dad was beside her. They were on an airplane, on their way at last. Sal glared at the seat in front of her as though her mixed-up feelings were all its fault.

"Are you crazy?" she asked herself fiercely. "You couldn't be scared of HOME!"

She twisted around to look at her father, but he was no help. He had fallen asleep. Leaning back in the seat, with his eyes closed, he seemed almost like a stranger. Sal shivered. Then, with a sigh of relief, she thought of the picture Mother had sent to her.

She burrowed into her coat pocket and dug out her wallet at once. She had looked at the snapshot so often that, once she got the wallet unfastened, it flipped open to the right place immediately. There they were—her family—Mother, Dad, Melinda, Kent and Meg.

Her father was lounging up against the porch pillar, his hair blowing up into little tufts, his glasses crooked, his grin wide. He looked more like himself in the picture, Sal thought, than he did asleep sitting so close to her that his sleeve touched hers.

Mother was sitting on the steps. The wind couldn't muss her long black hair pulled smoothly back into its bun, but it did fluff the short locks. She was smiling only a little, but Sally's breath caught as she felt the love in that smile. It was as though Mother reached a hand out of the picture and touched her gently, as though she said, in her special way, "Hi, Sarah Jane."

Mindy had moved just as the picture was taken, but you could see her head held high, her pony tail whisking through the air. She looked very grown-up.

Sal laughed as she looked at Kent. Whenever anyone took a snapshot of him, he insisted on standing like a Mountie on guard duty, as stiff as a poker, without the least hint of a smile on his face.

No matter how you posed Meg, on the other hand, she always looked like herself and nobody else. She was on Mother's knee, this time, but she sat a-straddle as though Mother were her horse. All Sal's doubts melted away, for a moment, as she looked down at her little sister, so full of mischief and charm.

Slowly, she started to put the wallet away, but just before it closed, she caught sight of the card on which she had printed her name and her home address when this wallet had been new:

Name: SARAH JANE COPELAND
Address: 43 VICTORIA STREET, RIVERSIDE, ONTARIO, CANADA

As she saw it, Sal's stomach lurched. She *was* scared, after all. It was no use scolding herself. She even began to see what was making her feel so strange and cold inside. It was all very well to wish and wish and *wish* to go home to live, when you were sure you wouldn't really have to do it. But once such a wish came true, it meant leaving the life you were used to and beginning a new one full of unfamiliar places and people.

Even home itself would be strange. A month ago, the Copelands had left that old two-storied brick house on Victoria Street and had moved to a new house she had never even seen. They had moved for her sake. Their new house was close to the Riverside Treatment Center for Children with Motor Handicaps, where she would be going for her therapy. But it wouldn't seem like home sleeping there tonight. Without everyone running around getting in each other's way, it wouldn't seem like home at all!

Why, she was remembering school, not the other house! Even though she had admitted to herself that she was afraid home would be different, she had not seen till now how much school had grown to seem like a home to her.

It wasn't just the girls either. Room 9 itself had become more Sally's home than the place where she spent her holidays. She knew exactly how it looked early in the morning when the other three girls were asleep and everything was still.

What with sixty children and nearly as many people on the staff, school was only quiet when almost everyone was asleep.

It was anything but quiet at night in that room, with Miss Jonas and the helpers trying to hustle them all into bed at once. "Lights Out" rang at half past eight and there never seemed to be quite enough time to finish before that bell. People hurried everywhere, helping to undo buttons and brush teeth, taking children to the toilet, bringing them back, dodging wheelchairs, unbuckling braces and giving orders which went unheard in the uproar. Miss Jonas's uniform snapped and swished as she strode from one to another. She would disappear into one of the other three rooms on their corridor and, just when you started clowning, she'd be right back beside you inquiring in an icy voice why you did not have your pajamas buttoned yet. They were all supposed to dress and undress themselves if they could, but whenever Miss Jonas had her back turned, Sal could get one of the helpers to whisk a few buttons undone for her.

The thought of getting ready for bed in a strange house, the thought of facing days without a bell to tell her when to do things, the thought of not having the other girls around, suddenly piled up into what looked like a mountain of troubles to Sally. Not one of those girls had been the special friend she had always longed to have, but just the same she would miss them terribly. Why, she would even miss Miss Jonas!

She gave a small miserable sniffle and Dad opened his eyes.

"Why didn't you poke me awake?" he said, stretching. "I guess I should have let Meg come for you after all."

"MEG!" Sal cried.

"Sure. Yesterday she told us that she was coming to get

you. Mindy asked her how she thought she'd go about it, and she said coolly, 'I'll drive down in one of those jets. They go like a car and anybody can drive a car, you know!' "

Sal laughed. That was Meg all right. She always was sure she knew everything there was to know about anything.

"I hope you won't mind sharing a room with Meg in the new house," Dad went on. "Somebody had to double up and we decided that you and Meg were the best pair. Melinda has a lot of homework to do now, and Kent has to have something to make up for him being the only boy, with three sisters."

Sal assured him she wouldn't mind. So she wasn't going to have to sleep in a room all alone! She made a little face at herself for having worried as though she were still small enough to be frightened of the dark. Still, her heart felt light suddenly, for she could not remember a time when there had not been someone sleeping in the room with her. Even on holidays in the old house, she had slept with Melinda. Now, in this new room she had never seen, at least Meg would be there.

"Look," Dad said. "We're coming down. There's Malton."

They were the last ones to leave the plane. The stewardess took Sal's crutches while Dad reached in and got Sally herself. He took his time and was careful not to bump their heads on the low ceiling the way he had when they got on. It seemed a long way to the car, but Dad strolled along as though he did not notice that Sal was slowing him down; and when she tried to go faster, he put his hand on her shoulder and said teasingly, "What's the rush? Don't you like taking a walk with a good-looking man?"

For the first twenty miles, she sat upright beside him watching the ribbon of road unrolling ahead of them. She thought of school, but switched her thoughts away when she realized that there, everybody would be in bed by now and her bed was standing empty. Once more, she tried to imagine the new house, but it was no use. She still kept seeing the old brick house she had always known.

Finally she drifted off to sleep, her head lolling over onto Dad's shoulder. She stayed that way until the car stopped, wakening her. Before she could get herself collected enough to remember where she was, the door beside her was flung open and her mother's arms closed about her in a long, tight hug.

"Oh, Sal honey, I'm so happy you're home!" her mother's voice half-sang right into her ear.

Sal blinked, and then hugged Mother back hard, as though she planned to hold on to her forever.

"Me too," she said—and the queer feeling was gone.

2

The New Room

"HI, SALLY," a sweet, small voice was saying, over and over and over.

Sal opened her eyes. Meg stood by her bed, rocking back and forth on her bare feet as she chanted her greeting. She was dressed in an old pair of Kent's pajamas. She had her hands planted on her hips. Her hair was tousled, her big hazel eyes shining. "She's just the same," Sal thought happily.

Meg suddenly came to with a jolt.

"You're awake!" she accused.

Before Sal could answer, her little sister was at the bedroom door shouting the news to everyone living on the block.

"SHE'S AWAKE!! SALLY'S AWAKE!"

At once it sounded as though at least a dozen people were hurrying to the spot. A boy's voice yelled, "Wowie!" Two doors slammed in different parts of the house. Somewhere, water was turned off; and from every direction came footsteps. Startled and excited, Sal watched the door. Mother reached it first. She fixed Meg with a withering look the minute she crossed the threshold.

"Margaret Ann Copeland," she started in sternly, using Meg's whole name to show how serious a matter it was, "I thought I told you quite clearly to leave Sally alone this morning. She was up late last night and she needed to sleep."

Meg defended herself stoutly.

"I never even touched her, did I, Sally? I was just standing looking at her—and she opened her eyes up all by herself, didn't you, Sally?"

Mother was not fooled by this, but she smiled in spite of herself.

Then Melinda and Kent came to the rescue, arriving in the doorway together. Mindy elbowed her way in first. She dived at Sal, giving her a hug and a kiss that left her breathless.

"It's about time you came home," she announced.

Not so ready with words, Kent snapped a salute at Sal from across the room. Then he swung himself up on top of the nearest dresser and perched there to watch whatever happened next.

Last of all, Dad sauntered in, making the family complete.

"Good morning, Miss Copeland," he said solemnly.

"Hi!" Sal got out, grinning at him.

Melinda and Mother were sitting on the two beds. Kent was still aloft on the chest of drawers and Dad leaned up against the doorjamb. Meg, too excited to settle, danced and hopped from one to the other. My whole family, Sal thought, looking around at them all; and then, without any warning, they were all looking at her! Suddenly, the room seemed jammed with people. Ten eyes fixed on her, all in one moment like that, were more than Sally could handle. She gave them back one frantic look. Then she went very red and felt a lump as big as a golfball come into her throat. They were waiting for her to say something—and that lump was so big she could not have gotten one word out, even if she had known what to say.

Mother saved her.

"How do you like your new room, Sarah Jane?" she asked, gesturing so that everyone's eyes were drawn away from Sal to the bedroom where they were gathered.

Nor did Mother stop there. She went on telling about the troubles she had had in getting just the right material for the drapes. She had asked for yellow drapes, "daffodil" or "buttercup" or even "dandelion," and the store sent "pea-soup green" and "parsnip" and "mustard."

Mindy interrupted to announce eagerly that she had chosen the wallpaper; and, from then on, Sal could relax. Every single one of them had some story to tell. Each corrected the others and, between them, they filled in a dozen funny details that soon had Sal shaking with laughter.

Just as the paperhanger was putting on the wallpaper, Meg had walked under it and had almost been pasted on along with it. "We were nearly rid of her that time, Sally," Dad said, sighing at the way things had turned out. Meg stuck out her tongue at him in reply. When the closets were being painted and the dressers had not arrived, Melinda had almost given all of Sal's and Meg's clothes away to a lady who had come around collecting for the Used Clothing Drive. "Well, how was I to know?" asked Mindy. "There was that big heap of clothes in the hall. I just naturally thought Mother had put them there on purpose." Kent had tried to help the electricians do the wiring and, as Dad put it, he had come "shockingly" close to being electrocuted.

Under cover of their chatter, Sal's blush faded. The lump in her throat melted away. Now, with unabashed delight, she sat and stared around her new room.

It was a big, square room with a southwest window to catch the afternoon sun and a southeast window through which the morning sun now poured. The drapes were yellow and so were the tiny flowers in the wreaths on the wallpaper and the sheepskin rug between the beds. There was a huge bookcase, the top shelves filled with her favorite books, the bottom shelves full of her old favorites which now belonged to Meg. And there was the tall mirror which had always stood in her parents' room in the old house. Sal had never paid much attention to it before, but now she liked it at once. It stood between the two dressers and it had an old frame, curiously carved.

Her family was still talking but Sal had stopped hearing what they said. She smiled, almost shyly, at the small bright flowers in the wallpaper. She turned her head and imagined herself sitting in the captain's chair, over by the window, reading maybe. She picked out which dresser was hers by her brush and comb, which Mother had already unpacked. "This is my room," she said to herself, to see how it sounded. "Mine and Meg's."

"Do you like it, Sarah Jane?" Mother asked, gently.

Sal just looked at her. It took a moment for her to come back from her own thoughts and understand what Mother meant.

"Your room, silly," Mindy prodded, an impatient note in her voice.

"Easy there, Melinda," Mother warned. "I'll do my own asking."

Mindy flushed and was quiet and Sal suddenly came to life.

"It's a beautiful room," she cried. "It's . . . it's beautiful!"

"It's my beautiful room too," Meg put in, sounding not quite sure.

"Of course it's yours too, funnyface. Now, I want every one of you to clear out of here and finish dressing. Breakfast will be ready in fifteen minutes. No comics in the bathroom, Kent. Move over, Andrew. Let them through."

Dad grinned at Mother, took Melinda and Kent each by a shoulder and marched them off down the hall singing "Three Blind Mice" off key. Mother laughed and picked up Sally's braces.

As she began to help Sal into them, Meg put down the sock she had just picked up.

"Why do you have to wear that?" she asked finally.

Sal had known the question was coming. She waited for Mother to explain, but Mother was fitting the braces into the high shoes Sally wore and she paid no attention to Meg.

"Why do you, Sally?"

"Well . . . it's . . . I have to wear them so I can walk," Sal mumbled at last.

"Why?" Meg countered.

Sal hesitated.

"Why?" Meg repeated, a little louder, as though she imagined Sal had not heard the first time.

"Because," Sal snapped.

She knew that would not satisfy Meg, and she looked at her mother again, but Mother was still busy doing up buckles.

"Because why?" came the inevitable small voice.

Sal thought hard. Until today, somebody else had always explained for her.

"Because I have cerebral palsy. It makes you so you can't walk and maybe your hands don't work just right. It makes you kind of stiff."

Then, remembering Bonnie and Alice, Jane Ann and Hilary, she stopped. All of them had cerebral palsy—and yet every single one of them showed it in a different way. Bonnie only limped a bit with her left leg. Alice could not walk but sat in a wheelchair all the time, with her arms and legs bent up and jerking. Jane Ann used crutches, but they were short wrist crutches. They didn't go up under your armpits like Sally's. And Hilary walked without much trouble, but she could not use a fork or a pencil or turn a doorknob or brush her own teeth because her hands were so involved. Then there was Louise, who could walk and use her hands fairly well, but had a terrible time talking. You had to know her for a long time before you could understand what she was trying so hard to tell you. She had cerebral palsy too. Memories of other children crowded into Sally's mind, confusing her still further. They all had cerebral palsy; and yet it suddenly seemed to her that there were dozens of different handicaps among them. She stared helplessly at Meg's waiting face.

Mother caught her expression of dismay and laughed.

"You're right, Sally. Cerebral palsy is pretty complicated. Just the same, I think you and Meg both could understand it better than you do. But, if you don't mind, let's wait till next weekend. You have an appointment then with Dr. Eastman in Toronto, and we'll take Meg along. I could explain, but he told Mindy about it when we first found out you had it and he did such a good job I'd like to see him do it again. Also, right this minute, everybody else in this house is just about ready for breakfast!"

She got up and fetched some clothing from Sal's dresser and the closet.

"Try these on for size, honey." She laid them within Sal's reach and smiled down at her. "You'll find the clothes are brand-new—to match your new room."

Then, without another word, she walked out.

Sal lay very still and stared after her. In one frightened instant, the safe warm feeling which had been growing inside her since Mother first hugged her the night before vanished.

Why, she couldn't dress herself! There were always slippery little blouse buttons impossible to do up and zippers with metal tabs so small your fingers couldn't keep hold of them! Didn't Mother know that? At school, there was always somebody there to help with the hard parts no matter what Miss Jonas said.

Sal lay very still. She lay and watched the door through which Mother had disappeared. Underneath all the arguments about buttons and zippers and school, she could hear another voice shouting: *She didn't even ask! She just left me! She's not ever going to stay! She doesn't care! She just left! She just left me all alone!*

"Aren't you going to get dressed now, Sally?"

Sal looked away from the door. She had forgotten Meg. How small and sure of herself she looked, sitting cross-legged on the floor, tugging on her socks. Sal almost smiled. Then she knew Meg was no help. She was too small. She couldn't take the place of a whole schoolful of girls with cerebral palsy. She couldn't drive away the fear that now surrounded Sally.

With a jerk, Sal rolled away from her little sister to face the wall, her braces clanking together. A giant sob ached in her throat. As her first tears wet the pillow under her cheek, she took back the wish she had been making so faithfully for such a long time, the wish "come true" just last night. In spite of the feeling she had had when Mother hugged her in the car, in spite of the beautiful room, in spite of Meg, in spite of all the years of waiting and wanting to go home to stay, Sally wanted to go back, back to where she was known and safe and never left alone for a minute. She wanted to go back to school!

3
Scarey Sarey

"DON'T CRY!" Meg begged, her voice shrill with alarm. "I'll get Mother. Don't cry, Sally!"

Sal wept on; and Meg scurried off to get help. She always ran to Mother with her own tears. By some special magic, Mother knew every time whether to cure them with a Band-Aid, a cooky or a kiss. Sal, crying into her pillow, was counting on Mother in much the same way.

"Thank you, honey. Now take your clothes to the kitchen and Melinda will help you."

Sal stiffened. There she was now. There. That was Meg leaving. Now Mother would come over and take her in her arms and everything would be all right again. Still lying with her face to the wall, Sal sniffed loudly and sorrowfully. Then she held her breath and waited.

Footsteps crossed the room. There was a creaking sound over by Meg's bed. Far away, Sal heard dishes clinking together and Mindy's voice giving an order. Then a door closed and silence fell. Nothing moved. Nobody spoke. Nothing at all happened.

Sal was stunned. Surely Mother had come in! Yes, of course she had! She had heard her talking to Meg. She had even heard her walking across the room. So why didn't she do something . . . or say something!

Sally gulped. She couldn't look. She was certain that Mother hadn't left the room. But if she were doing anything at all, she would make a noise. And there was no noise.

The answer came to her suddenly. Mother probably thought she was asleep. She must be being extra quiet so as not to waken her. Sal sniffed again; but this time the sniff was very small and uncertain.

At once, the silence swallowed it.

Sal waited. There was nothing else she could think of to do. A minute passed. It seemed an hour. She began to feel sure someone was watching her. Another minute passed, and another. She stuck it out for one more long, long minute. Then, with a gasp, she turned over.

Mother was sitting on Meg's bed.

"That's better," she said quietly, as Sal stared at her. "I'm not in the habit of talking to people's backs. Now suppose you tell me what your trouble is."

Sal was so taken aback she couldn't think of a word to say. Then she found herself in the middle of another silence.

"Don't you know I can't do it all by myself?" she burst out, new tears streaming down her face.

"Do what all by yourself?" Mother asked evenly.

Never had Sarah Jane Copeland felt more muddled and miserable. Once again, silence began to press in on her, but how could she explain to Mother while Mother sat looking so calm and far-off!

"All those buttons, that's what!" she shouted, glaring.

At last, the questions stopped.

"Sally, I have a story to tell you," Mother said.

She tucked her feet up under her as though she had all the time in the world. A little of the fear went out of Sally.

"One summer there was a four-year-old girl who had an older sister and a brother just turned two. Her parents packed up their three children and some clothes and rented a cottage by Lake Huron for one week. The moment they arrived, they all got into their bathing suits, even the baby, and went down to the lake to swim."

Sal said nothing. Her eyes were dark and startled.

"They had been afraid they might have to coax the baby into the water," Mother went on, "but he ran right into it as though it were his bath at home. It was very shallow, so his mother wasn't worried. She just stayed close to him and watched. When the waves hit him, he tried to catch them in his fists and he laughed as though it were a game. The older girl went in more slowly. She put one toe in and squealed 'OooooooOOOOOOOO, it's COLD!' But before long she was in up to her neck. Only the little four-year-old girl did not join in and have fun with the others. She began to scream as soon as she saw the water. She buried her head in her father's shoulder and, no matter what anyone said, she wouldn't let even her toes be put into the lake."

Mother paused, but Sal was still silent.

"The little girl's family stayed at the lake for a week. Every day the whole family went in swimming—all but the little girl. Every day, her daddy told her how nice it was, but she wouldn't listen. He waded in to show her how shallow it was, but she wouldn't look. The little girl's name was Sarah, and soon they began to call her 'Scarey Sarey' and tease her for being so silly, but still, Sarah wouldn't have anything to do with that water.

"On the next to the last day, her father grew tired of coaxing. He knew that, by then, Sarah had herself so scared she'd never go in unless someone made her. So he picked her up and carried her in."

Sal's tears had dried on her cheeks. She remembered that day. It was so long ago it seemed almost a dream, but she could still feel the way she had clutched at Dad and shrieked as he had walked to the lake.

"Her father tried to be gentle"—Mother remembered too—"but Scarey Sarey cried and fought, so at last he had to just pull her hands loose and put her down and leave her. It was so shallow it wasn't dangerous. And since Sarah couldn't walk, she had to stay there whether she wanted to or not. Maybe you remember what happened, Sally, when that little girl stopped crying long enough to notice what the water was really like."

Sal nodded slowly. It did not seem like a dream any longer. The lake had been calm that day. Greenish ripples had broken softly against her. Kent had crowed with excitement and galloped around her, churning up a frothy sparkle. Nearby, Mother had been holding Mindy on her stomach, making her "swim" on top of the bright water. Suddenly giving in completely, she, Sal, had called to Dad, "I want to swim too. Make me swim like Mindy, Daddy."

"Five long days at the beach—wasted!" remarked Mother, as though Sally had spoken her memories aloud. "Five days wasted because Scarey Sarey didn't wait to find out whether there was anything to cry about before she started crying. . . . But, of course, she was only four. You can forgive a little girl like that for not taking time to think."

Sal blushed, a slow, deep, burning blush right up to her ears. She looked at the rug.

"Have you really looked at the clothes I put out for you to wear this morning, Sal?"

Unable to speak, Sal only shook her head. Mother rose and

reached for the clothes. One piece at a time, she spread them out across Sal's knees.

"Now show me those buttons you're so worried about!"

With her head bent and her heart thumping uncomfortably, Sal inspected the clothing. The expression on her face grew more and more sheepish as she looked.

There were no buttons. Not a single button anywhere! In fact, the clothes on her lap were the simplest clothes to put on that Sal had ever seen. The skirt was full with an elasticized top. No zipper! No tricky fastening at all! And the soft yellow blouse had a wide boat neck with a rolled-over collar. No hooks and eyes! No skimpy little puffed sleeves! Even the underwear was specially made with generous openings for arms and legs. All the things that made dressing difficult were missing—and yet the clothes themselves looked lovely.

"I — I'm sorry. They're wonderful clothes," Sal gulped.

Mother dropped down on the bed beside her and circled Sal lightly with her arms.

"Sally, Sally, don't be so afraid," she said softly. "If not being able to do up buttons were all that was troubling you, you wouldn't be wanting to cry again this minute. You're scared to death that I'm going to walk out and leave you with nobody to look after you. Don't you know that I would never do that if I didn't know, for certain sure, that you didn't need me?"

Astonishment held back Sal's tears. How could Mother see inside a person's thoughts like that?

"Now guess who suggested those new clothes for you."

"You must have," Sal faltered.

"Wrong. Miss Jonas did."

"MISS JONAS!"

"Miss Jonas. When you left Allendale, she wrote us a long letter about you. You'd be surprised at some of the things she knows about you, Sarah Jane. Most important, she told us that if we all, including you, started working on it right away, there will come a day when you, Sal Copeland, will be an independent adult. An independent adult is a person who decides things for herself and does things for herself and for others. It would mean having your own job, your own friends, your own money, your freedom."

To Sal it sounded frightening and far off, but fun too. Her own friends! She had wanted a special friend badly for a long time now.

"But to be independent someday means beginning practicing independence *today;* and the first step is dressing yourself. Only, before you begin, I'm going to cut your hair."

Sal had thought she was past feeling surprised, but Mother's announcement knocked the breath clean out of her. *Cut her hair!* Why, she'd had long pigtails ever since she could remember. Miss Jonas had braided them every morning and neither she nor Carla, who also had them, had dared so much as squeak when she raked the snarls out with a strong hand. Surely her mother didn't really mean to . . .

Twenty minutes later, Mother stood back, looked over her handiwork one last time, and declared it was perfect. The floor was littered with long strands of wheat-colored familiar-looking hair. Gingerly, Sal put up a hand to feel what was left, but Mother batted her exploring fingers down.

"None of that," she ordered. "No looking in the mirror, either. Here are your clothes. Get yourself dressed. Then you can see your whole new self at once. Now get busy."

She hoisted Sal back to the bed, from the captain's chair

where she had sat to have her hair cut, put her crutches within reach, and left.

For one long moment, Sal sat and stared down at the clothes beside her. Then she began to move. She hitched the short nightgown out from under her and hauled it over her head. For the first time, she noticed that it was new and different too, like the other clothes. Only the gay up and down stripes saved it from looking like a plain sack with holes in it for her head and arms.

But it was too cold in the room to sit in her bare skin and admire it. If she didn't get into something quickly, she'd freeze.

Just the same, frozen or thawed, it took a long time. Wriggling into and tugging at each garment in turn soon had her puffing and red in the face. Her fingers, always a little awkward, seemed to stiffen on purpose to make things harder. She put her arm through the hole in her blouse which was meant for her head and it took ages to pull it free again. The skirt twisted itself around her legs and, however hard she yanked at it, it refused to straighten out. More than once, she came close to giving up, but something about that "Scarey Sarey" story kept her going doggedly until she was done.

She looked down at herself and drew a sharp little breath of excitement. She had managed it! She was dressed. She wriggled forward until her feet were firmly on the floor and reached for her crutches. Leaning down, she got her braces locked and then put her weight solidly on the handgrips. After trying a couple of times, she was up. Holding her breath, she turned and started for the mirror.

Without warning, the door swung wide and the other Copelands crowded in. Forever afterwards, Sal was to wonder whether they had been watching her through the keyhole.

"Is that Sally?" Meg asked, her eyes round.

Kent gave a wolf whistle, and Mindy breathed "Gee!"

"Hush," Mother said. "Let her see for herself."

Shyly, shakily, Sally approached the glass. As she caught sight of herself, she stopped in her tracks. Even though she had known she would be different, she was totally unprepared for this girl in the mirror.

Sal was not used to seeing herself in a looking glass. At school she had practiced walking in front of one, but the therapist had always been telling her to watch her knees or keep her elbows in. Over the years, Sally had grown to look at herself a piece at a time. She had come to have a vague picture of herself, a girl all elbows and knees and crutches, with a face and clothes too ordinary to notice much.

This was a new Sally.

She was dressed in bright, soft colors. In place of the long braids she wore a smooth shining cap of hair with no part at all. It was almost as short as a boy's, but it had bangs straight across the front and it curved in just a little on the ends. From all her hard work, and excitement, her cheeks glowed like roses. In spite of herself, her mouth tipped up in a delighted smile and her blue eyes shone bluer than ever with wonder.

Sal glanced away from the glass at her family. At the admiration on their faces, her cheeks grew rosier.

"I look like somebody else," she half-whispered at last. "Not me."

"Somebody beautiful," smiled Dad, and bowed to her with a flourish.

4

Nobody Likes Piet

THE REST of that first Saturday flew by. There was Mindy's cat, Purrpuss, to play with, Kent's chestnut collection to admire and Meg's questions to answer. In the afternoon, Mother took her exploring through every nook and cranny of the new house. She showed Sal chairs in every room which had rubber tips on their legs so that she would be able to lower herself into them or hoist herself up out of them without having them skid away from her. The sheepskin rug beside her bed, too, had had foam rubber sewn onto its underside to keep it firmly in place when she placed her crutch on it. Last but not least, Sally discovered that all the clothes in her closet and dresser were like those Mother had given her that morning—easy to put on, and yet pretty too.

That night, before she went to sleep, Sal thought about the day. If she had only waited a little longer, looked a bit further, trusted Mother more, she wouldn't have been Scarey Sarey over again and started off with tears.

"Nothing," she vowed, there in the darkness, "will ever make me a baby like that again. Nothing!"

The next afternoon, she broke her resolution. The dinner dishes were done and the family was gathering in the living room. Dad and Kent were already busy with a gigantic jigsaw puzzle. Mindy sat down at the piano and started leafing through the music. Mother picked up her sewing, and Sal opened her book only to find Meg at her elbow.

"Read to me, Sally," Meg demanded. "Read me my Babar book."

Sal groaned. She had already read about Babar three times in the last two days. Besides, she wanted to read to herself.

"Tomorrow, Meg," she answered. "I promise I'll read it to you then."

"My dear young lady, tomorrow you'll be in school with Melinda and Kent."

It was Mother's voice speaking, but several seconds passed before Sally realized that it was speaking to her. School! Why, she had just left Allendale the day before yesterday! And she wouldn't be going with Mindy and Kent, anyway. She would be going to a special class for handicapped children at the Center.

"I thought Sally was going to go to school at the Center," Mindy said, twirling about on the piano stool so that she faced them and speaking Sal's thoughts aloud. "Do you mean to say she'll be coming to Princess Elizabeth with us?"

Mother was biting off a thread so she could only nod her head. She looked at Sally as she did so, but Sal's eyes, staring back at her, went suddenly blank. The book she had been holding slipped from her hands.

"Honey," Mother said, but her voice was drowned in the excited uproar which had sprung up around them.

"It's a great school!" Kent deserted the jigsaw to tell his sister, not noticing her failure to answer.

"You'll be in Mr. Mackenzie's class," Melinda said at the same minute. "They say he's a wonderful teacher. I think

Janice's sister is in his room and I know Jon Nordway is in there. He's a darling little boy. You'll just love him, Sally."

Kent hooted.

"'A darling little boy'!" he mimicked. "If Jon could hear you, he'd strangle you with his bare hands. Gee whiz, Mindy. He's a good kid! I know lots of other kids in that class: Jeff Jorgenson, Randy, and George. And of course, there's His Majesty the Show-off's sister!"

"Whose sister?" everyone but Sal asked.

Kent began clowning at once. He struck a grand pose, swept a bow so deep it almost toppled him over, and chanted at the top of his lungs:

Piet, Piet,
Fat as a beet,
Size Two head
And Size Ten feet!

"That's whose sister!"

"Son," Dad began, but Kent was making so much noise he did not even hear him. He strutted around the room, his nose in the air.

"Haven't you heard of Piet?" he asked loudly, "His Majesty, King Pieter, Ruler of all Holland and . . . and . . . lots of other places around there. Why, he's so special he says his name's Peter but you have to spell it with an extra letter! He's so special he can't even talk English! It's too ordinary for him. He's so wonderful . . ."

"That's enough, Kent," Dad said sharply.

"But, Dad," Kent began, "*nobody* likes Piet!"

Then, he saw his father's expression and was quiet.

"Who is this boy you have been telling us about?" Dad asked.

"Pieter Jansen." The answer came in a low voice.

Dad had come over to sit on the arm of the couch. Now he reached out and took Kent by the shoulders so that Kent had to face him.

"You don't like Pieter," he said. "But that does not give you the right to make fun of the fact that he cannot speak English as well as you can. Does he come from Holland?"

"Yes, sir."

"Let's hear you speak some Dutch."

There was a long silence. Kent stared at his shoes. Mother, watching Sal, saw that her face had lost that look of emptiness it had worn a few moments before. Sal was so sorry for Kent that she had stopped being afraid for herself. Also, for some queer reason she did not understand, she found herself wanting to know more about this boy Piet whom nobody liked.

"All right, son. You get my point. Sometimes it is hard to like people, but to mock someone, as you just did—that hurts you, Kent, far worse than it hurts the person you mock. I hope I never hear you do it again. Now, what was it you were telling us about Piet's sister?"

Very little of Kent's bounce was left as he muttered, "Her name is Alice or Elsie or something like that. She's in Mr. Mackenzie's room. She'll be in Sally's class in school."

Dad glanced at Sal and smiled. Then he turned back to Kent.

"Let's finish that puzzle, boy," he said.

"Will you read me my Babar book now, Sally?" Meg asked, hopefully.

"No, she won't," Mother answered for Sally. "Melinda will read it to you and you will take it somewhere else to read it. I want to talk to Sal for a minute."

"MOTHER!" Mindy protested, glaring at Meg.

"MELINDA!" Mother said right back at her with a smile, but the look she gave Mindy was firm, and a moment later, Meg and Melinda were gone.

"I didn't mean to spring it on you like that, honey," Mother said. "But it is true. They have a full class at the Center without you and your teachers at Allendale think you are ready to be transferred to a regular elementary school. Miss Jonas thinks so too."

"Miss Jonas doesn't know anything about schoolwork," Sal muttered.

"She knows a lot about you, though. She says that you'll find out how to make friends of your own and that you will learn more about life than you could ever learn in a school which is only for children with handicaps like yours."

But in all Sal's life, she had never been in a classroom where the children were not handicapped.

"If going to a regular school is so wonderful, why didn't you send me to one all along?" she cried desperately.

Sal was not thinking clearly at all. She just had a feeling, a terrifying feeling of being pushed out into a world full of strangeness, of being pushed into a world she was not ready to meet.

"Now just a minute, Miss Sarah Jane Copeland," Mother said. There was a sudden spark in her brown eyes and a decided snap in her voice. All at once, Dad sauntered over.

"My turn to say a few words," he interrupted.

At the sound of his voice, slow and easy, the starch went out of Mother's spine and the fire left her eyes. Even Sal felt calmer and prepared to listen.

"You want to know why we sent you away to school," Dad said, settling himself between them on the couch. "Well, Sal, you were Meg's age, but you couldn't feed yourself. You couldn't help to undress yourself. You couldn't talk clearly enough so that strangers could understand you. Of course, we could have kept you at home and looked after you. We loved you. We didn't mind dressing you and feeding you, and we understood you. But we thought you'd rather be able to do these things for yourself. How about it? Were we right?"

Sal did not want to answer, but he waited. At last, not looking at him, she gave a very small nod. She could still remember little bits from those days when she had had to have everything done for her. Once she had wanted very badly to help Kent build a block house, but when she had wriggled close and had put out her hand, she had knocked all the blocks down.

"Thank you for approving," Dad said, his face serious. "We would have asked you, but you were a little young at the time. We did think of moving to a big city instead, but I had my business here and we thought that we would have a treatment center built long before this. We sent you to the best school we could afford and we worked hard toward persuading the community to build a treatment center, and the moment the Center was built we fetched you home. What would you have done differently?"

His question caught Sal off guard.

"I . . . I don't know. I guess . . . you had to," she mumbled.

"But this isn't getting at what's really bothering you, is it?" Dad said gently. "What's got you scared silly is this school you're going to tomorrow."

Kent suddenly lost interest in the puzzle as he stared at his father and at Sally.

"It's a great school, I told you," he said accusingly.

"To listen to him you'd never dream that last month he was raising the roof about going there, would you? Mindy too! They swore nobody would like them. Nobody would even speak to them. They were *sure* they'd hate it. Why, oh, why couldn't we move back to the old house where they knew everybody and his little brother? And two days later—guess what, Sarah Jane?"

"What?" Sal asked, unwillingly.

"There were kids spilling out of the windows. The telephone never rang for me any longer. 'Melinda Copeland, if you please,' as one of her new friends always says. The only time we ever saw Kent was when he dropped by to eat. For two friendless people, your brother and sister were remarkably busy."

Sal scrunched down on the couch and did not laugh. Anybody would know that Mindy and Kent would find friends. She *was* different.

"Sally, sit up and listen to your father," her mother ordered.

"She is listening, Emily. She just doesn't think it applies to her, that's all. She thinks she's different, don't you, Sal?"

Sal glared at him. She was getting sick and tired of people reading her thoughts. She didn't just *think* she was different. She *was* different.

"You're quite right," her father said, taking her hand. "In one small detail, you are different. You have a motor handicap.

That seems like a lot more than a small detail to you though."

"It sure does," Sal's voice was hoarse with feeling. She tried to pull her hand free but Dad held it fast.

"But, Sal, don't you see that the real you, the you that matters, has nothing to do with your braces or crutches?" he asked her, leaning forward and speaking to her as though he felt these were the most important words that had ever been said between them. "Your laugh, that's part of the real you. Your dreams and your ideas. Are you seriously trying to tell me that the girl you are underneath is some kind of freak that nobody can like?"

"NO!" Sal roared. "I'm not a freak. I'm just a girl. But I'll still be the only girl on crutches."

"You remember that you're just a girl and forget about the crutches and I guarantee everybody else will too," Dad promised her.

Sal wanted to believe him. They looked at each other, their eyes exactly the same noon-sky blue, his patient and strong, hers hopeful but still afraid.

"Nobody likes Piet," she blurted at last.

Dad did not seem surprised, although neither he nor she had ever heard of Pieter Jansen before that afternoon, as far as she knew.

"Maybe Piet never gave them a chance," her father said quietly.

5

Too Many Faces

"MOTHER, WAIT!" Sal whispered urgently.

Mother, who had taken a step closer to the classroom door, stopped. She looked down at Sal understandingly.

"Honey, Mr. Mackenzie is expecting us and it's getting late. Let's get it over with," she said firmly.

She put her hand on Sal's shoulder, urging her forward with a gentle push. Sal, already in a panic, did her best to back away. At that moment the door flew open. A girl came shooting through it and collided head-on with Sally. Sal clutched wildly at thin air. Mother grabbed her from behind. The crutches skidded across the hall. And the girl went down on both knees at Sally's feet, with a look of intense astonishment on her face.

"Oh my!" she gasped.

She scrambled up, her cheeks as red as poppies.

"You're Sally Copeland!" she cried. "Oh, I'm sorry. . . . Your crutches!"

She dived after them while Mother got Sal balanced. Then, as Sally was getting her crutches adjusted, she ordered off four or five children who had gathered to see what was going on. At last, with Sal standing straight again and the children dispersed, the girl relaxed. She smiled widely.

"I'm Libby Reeves," she introduced herself, her voice still a bit breathless.

Sal smiled back. She could not have helped it. Libby's smile, as anyone could tell you, was something special. So was the rest of her. Her short, curly hair was a flaming, carroty red. Her face was splattered with freckles. Her eyes were as green as grass. Her glasses, which had been knocked askew and now perched crookedly on her upturned nose, had been mended in three places. And she was the thinnest person that Sally had ever seen. Sal herself had been called "skinny," but Libby was nothing short of spidery, with long pipe-cleaner legs stretching down beneath the hem of her skirt and equally long bony arms which she kept waving about while she talked.

A nudge from Mother warned Sal not to stare, but Libby must have been used to it for she talked steadily on.

"Mr. Mackenzie said you'd start today and I was all ready to greet you but I didn't mean to give you such a knockdown welcome. Buddy was chasing me and I never thought someone would be standing right outside the door like that. My mother always says I act first and think second. I didn't hurt you, did I?"

"No, I'm fine." Sal's voice was rusty with shyness.

"Good. Oh, here's Mr. Mackenzie now. This is Sally Copeland, sir."

Mr. Mackenzie was tall with broad shoulders and a dark, kind face. As she shook hands with him, Sal stood straighter and felt braver.

"Libby, will you show Sal where to hang her coat, and then bring her to the classroom?" he asked.

Mother and he walked off together, talking, and Libby led the way to a row of lockers built into the wall.

"This will be yours," she said, opening the last one. "Elsje's and mine is down two."

Sal propped herself against the wall and began working her way out of her coat. Libby watched her uncertainly.

"Do you need any help?" she ventured at last.

"No," Sal answered, thankful there was just one, easy button, "I do it better sitting down but it's okay. Who's Elsje?"

"Elsje Jansen. She's my best friend. She's from Holland. Her family only came to Canada a little over a year ago but you should hear her speak English! She's really smart!"

Sal stayed balanced with one hand while she hung up her coat with the other. She kept her head down.

"Does she have a brother named Piet?"

"How did you know?" Libby said in surprise.

"Oh, my brother said something about a Piet Jansen going to this school," Sal answered vaguely.

It was no use thinking any more about being Libby's friend. Libby had just said herself that Piet's sister was her "best friend." Sally got herself balanced again on her crutches. A bit of the rhyme Kent had chanted about Piet sang inside her head.

Piet, Piet,
Fat as a beet . . .

"Here comes your mother."

Sal straightened, gripping the crosspieces of her crutches tightly. Mother reached the two girls and looked down into Sally's eyes. Sal was sure that she saw Scarey Sarey looking back at her, but she only gave Sal's shoulder a little squeeze and said:

"Behave yourself, Sarah Jane. We'll be waiting to hear all about it at lunch. 'By for now."

"Good-by."

It came out so faintly that Sal herself could scarcely hear it. Mother turned, walked briskly down the hall and vanished through a door at the far end. Sal did not move. Perhaps, she thought, if she just stayed absolutely still she would be safe.

Then Libby said "Come on," in a matter-of-fact voice, and Sal found herself following the other girl across the hall to the classroom door.

Libby in the lead, they went through the door and into the room itself. "Scarey Sarey" was everywhere, shouting at Sal to turn and run before it was too late, but she kept going like a small machine, her eyes glued to the middle of Libby's back, her braces and crutches clanking and thumping with every step she took. She had thought, for a moment, that just standing still in the hall would keep her safe. Now she was sure that the one thing she had to do was to go on looking at Libby. She must not make the mistake of raising her eyes, even for a split second . . .

"Here's your seat," Libby said, turning—and Sal looked up.

She was face to face with a roomful of strange children. After the first glance, some of them looked away uneasily, but many stared back at her, their eyes bright with curiosity. Sal did not stop to think that she had stared at Libby like this only a few minutes before. Too many faces, too many . . . she thought dizzily.

"Sally?"

Libby's smile, even though it was a little puzzled, acted like a lucky piece. Sal's eyes found it and everything that had been going wrong suddenly was right again.

"Thanks," she said.

Awkwardly, she turned herself sideways in the aisle. Libby backed up, out of the way of her crutches. Then, with an unexpected thud and a small feeling of victory, Sal took her seat.

For the next few minutes, she was too busy to notice whether anyone was staring at her or not. She had to get her crutches stowed out of the way, and then undo the knee-locks on her braces and get turned around so that her feet were under the desk instead of sticking out blocking the aisle. The lock on the left brace jammed. Sally tugged at it angrily. Her fingers, stiff with tension and damp with perspiration, slipped on the smooth steel. She wiped her palm on her skirt, gave one more tug, and the lock clicked open. Her knees bent. She swung her feet under her desk and sighed thankfully.

Never before had she noticed how much room she took up or how much noise she made, doing this simple thing. Never before had it seemed to take such a long time to get it done. But then, this was the first time she had ever done it in a schoolroom where others weren't doing it too.

Libby's whisper cut through her thoughts.

"Hey, Sally, look. Here comes Elsje."

Sally looked. She saw a girl cross the front of the room, come down the aisle and slide into a chair near her own. Elsje was small, but sturdy, with square shoulders and a straight back. Her hair hung nearly to her waist in glossy braids, so neatly braided you might have thought that Miss Jonas had arranged that hair, Sal thought admiringly. Under a navy-blue jumper, Elsje wore a white blouse with long sleeves and a round collar. The collar made her look young. Yet there was something in her face that made Sal feel that Elsje was more grown-up than she was.

Libby had been scribbling busily on a piece of paper. Now she smiled at Sal and passed the note to Elsje. Piet's sister pulled absent-mindedly on one of her braids as she read what her friend had written.

It's about me, Sal thought—It's something about me!

Elsje finished reading. She folded the scrap of paper and shoved it out of sight into her desk. Then she lifted her head and looked at Sal. Sal stared back. Elsje looked as though she were facing up to a dragon in her path, instead of just another girl. Sal had no idea what was wrong, but the feeling in Elsje's eyes burned so fiercely that she drew back in spite of herself. At that, Elsje's expression changed. Her eyelids dropped for an instant. When they rose again, the glance she gave Sal was cold and hard. All the fire of a moment before was gone. Yet when Sal turned quickly away, she found that she could not make her hands stop shaking for a minute.

Don't be crazy! she told herself. She doesn't know you. You're just letting yourself be Scarey Sarey again!

Then she forced herself to look at the other girl once more. Elsje had turned away, but on her lap her hands were knotted together so tightly the knuckles were white. She was sitting stiffly, her shoulders strained back. Her face looked set as though she had somehow managed to turn her own bones and skin into a mask to hide what was happening in her heart. It had not been Scarey Sarey after all.

Clang!

A bell rang suddenly and every child in the room, except Sal, stood up. Sally stared wildly at the empty desks all around her and at the forest of plaid skirts, blue jeans, jumpers and slacks that had risen on every side. What was happening? Then they began to sing "God Save the Queen." She still did not know what to do. By the time she again got her braces locked, her crutches in place and herself standing, it would be finished and they would all sit down and leave her—the only child on her feet. She stayed where she was.

All through the "Queen" . . . All through the Lord's Prayer! She tried to sing and pray with them, but she couldn't. Then she just tried to look as though she didn't care. A smile, real enough to fool anybody, was more than she could manage.

Amen, the children around her murmured, and the class sat down.

"Boys and girls," Mr. Mackenzie said, when the rustling stopped, "I'd like you to meet the new member of our class, Sally Copeland."

Sal was pretending she was not there. She had not been sitting there through the opening exercises. She had never looked at Elsje. She had not even heard of Piet. She looked through Mr. Mackenzie instead of at him and she said inside herself *I am invisible,* but it didn't work.

"Sally, I'm sorry," the teacher said, his voice warm with amusement and sympathy. "We should have prepared you for 'God Save the Queen.' You must have wondered what on earth was happening when everybody jumped up like that. It won't be half as exciting coming to school tomorrow."

The children around Sal laughed. She sat very still trying not to hear that word "tomorrow." Mr. Mackenzie glanced at her and then went on easily:

"I'd introduce you to everybody, but you'd be more

muddled at the finish than you are right now. There are a few rascals, however, about whom somebody should warn you. Randy, for instance. If Randy offers to help you with your spelling, Sal, be polite, but say NO!"

The boys and girls laughed again as though they were used to his teasing and liked it. Sal smiled too. The boy Mr. Mackenzie was talking about had stuck his nose in the air and was pretending to be deeply hurt about the whole thing.

"Libby is an expert on how to have fun—even in school," the teacher went on. "And Elsje? Why, she is learning to speak English so well I have to study at night secretly so that she won't catch me making a mistake and have me fired!"

Stealing a look at Elsje, Sal could hardly believe this was the same girl. She actually dimpled as she protested, "No, no. I shall never be so good as that. Never!"

After that, it seemed that Sally's troubles were over. First the children wrote stories. When she had finished, Sal scowled down at hers for a moment. Some of the letters were thin, some fat, some almost too cramped to read, some sprawling. And the lines all went uphill instead of straight across the page. Then she read it over and her face cleared. Sal had always had fun writing stories. Mr. Mackenzie would understand that it was hard for her to handle a pencil easily.

She was through early and Libby brought her a library book to read. Sal sat beaming at the book. That must mean that Libby didn't care what Elsje thought.

They did spelling. The words were new to everybody. As they finished, Sal caught sight of the clock and realized with amazement that over an hour of the morning had gone.

It's all right, she thought joyfully. I'll soon be home.

And then they had the mental arithmetic test!

6

The Test

A BROWN-HAIRED, brown-eyed boy handed out blank sheets of paper. Sal looked down at hers uncertainly.

"There will be fifteen questions," Mr. Mackenzie's voice said from the other side of the room. "Don't forget to number your answers. Number 1: 4 plus 9."

Sally picked up her pencil hurriedly. Everybody else, used to these tests, had already put down Number 1 and was now writing the answer. Sal wrote the number of the question. Suddenly Mr. Mackenzie's voice boomed out: "Number 2: 17 minus 8."

Sal knew her arithmetic facts as well as most of the children in the room. But this way of checking them was new to her. By the time she got the first question answered, the class was dashing down the third answer and she did not even know what had been asked.

One swift glance around the room told Sal that nobody else was having the same trouble she was. She never stopped to think that her awkwardness with a pencil and the fact that the whole way of testing was unfamiliar to her could be to blame. She must be terribly far behind in arithmetic, she decided. Every pencil she could see was putting down one number under the next without stopping for a minute. Even if some of them were wrong, they at least were all writing something.

Sal hunched over her paper. Instinctively, she put her arm around it as a shield, so that no one would see how stupid she was. Trying to look as busy as the others, she printed the numbers of the questions. Number 8 was so easy—7 plus 7—that she stopped to scribble down the answer. But when she had it written, she found that the class had finished Number 9.

"Everybody ready?"

Sal stared down at the list of numbers from 1 to 15 with only two answers beside them.

"Fine. Today you can check your own work."

Now Mr. Mackenzie was reading the right answers—slowly, giving the children time to mark them. Still trying to look occupied, Sal copied them down in their proper places as he read them. Some of her figures were scrawled so badly that they were almost impossible to make out, but she got the complete list.

Later, when she tried to think through what had really happened, Sal could not remember stopping to plan what she did next. She just did it. In a queer daze that was half desperation, she moved her pencil to the top of the page once more and, carefully, she checked every answer written there, as though she had gotten all fifteen correct.

"Much better, Sharon," she heard Mr. Mackenzie saying. He was walking among the desks, collecting the sheets of answers. "Good for you, Bob. Mary Ellen, what happened to you?"

Then he was beside her desk. He was looking at her paper. As he stood there looking down at it, Sal saw, all at once, what she had done. He must see it too! Anyone could tell that the numbers of the questions had been written first and the answers were scribbled in later. She had cheated. Those check marks! Without those, maybe it would not be called cheating. But there they were!

Mr. Mackenzie laid his hand on her shoulder for a fraction of a second, picked up the sheet of paper, and went on.

I didn't get them right. I missed them all. You went too fast. I couldn't help it. I CHEATED! Sal shouted after him —but only in her mind.

She stared at the little streaks in the wood of her desk, at the green pencil lying there. That was the pencil she had used.

Far away a bell rang. Far away, a voice, Libby's voice, spoke to her.

"Come on, Sal. That bell means it's time for recess."

Slowly, Sal lifted her head. She felt heavy and sick all over.

What if I never do it again? she asked herself, not answering Libby, not even seeing her. I didn't mean to, this time. Maybe it doesn't count if you don't mean to, and you never do it again. I promise I won't ever do it again.

Libby was waiting. Elsje was there, too, standing just behind her. Sal reached for her crutches.

"I'm coming," she said, fighting to sound ordinary in spite of the ache in her throat.

Then Piet's sister spoke.

"You can play with her if you want to," Elsje said, her voice hard, "but I will not. I am not going to be friends with her. She lies!"

"Els, what are you talking about?" Libby cried.

Sal did not have to ask. Elsje knew. Elsje had seen her cheating. Now, Elsje was going to tell. Sally gave the girl who now faced her one imploring look, but the scorn in Elsje's eyes did not soften.

"Let her tell you herself," she said shortly. "She knows what I mean."

"Sal?" Libby questioned.

Libby's eyes were bewildered but they were still ready to be friendly.

"I . . ." Sal began, "I was . . ."

But there were no words for what she had done. Elsje had not told on her, but she had left her no escape, either, for Sal could not deny that she had cheated. She could not explain away something Elsje had seen.

All at once, Sal felt tears coming. But she couldn't cry now! Not in front of Elsje! Somehow she had to keep the hurt inside her hidden away from Elsje's mocking eyes—yes, and from Libby's pitying ones as well.

Just in time, she lost her temper. Anger went off inside her like a rocket. They hated her and she hated them right back. Her spine straightened and her eyes snapped.

"Why don't you mind your own business?" she heard herself say, in a new voice, as tough as Elsje's. "I'm not going to stay in this stupid school anyway. I wouldn't go to a dumb school like this even if you paid me. And I wouldn't be friends with you either, not for any money!"

"B . . . but, Sally!" Libby broke in, completely confused.

"Tell her what you did, why don't you?" taunted Elsje, in the same second.

"Elsje, don't." Libby still did not understand, but she was deeply troubled.

The other girl thrust out her chin defiantly. She turned away from Sal to face her old friend.

"Just look at her!" she cried. "She won't even say to you what she did that is wrong. I am leaving. If you want to stay with her, Libby, you are not my friend any longer!"

Her voice trembled on the last words but she wheeled about and stalked proudly up the aisle.

Libby stared after her. Then she looked at Sal, the new girl, the stranger. Sal returned her look as coldly as Elsje herself could have done it. She wasn't going to have any skinny redhead feeling sorry for her!

"I've got to go with her, Sal," Libby said unhappily. "She's my best friend. I'm sorry."

The anger which had shot through Sal with all the bright, flaring unexpectedness of a rocket deserted her as suddenly as it had come. Before Libby had quite reached the door, she was searching her pocket for the handkerchief Mother had given her that morning. There was no time to pillow her head on her arms and weep the way she longed to do. She mopped her cheeks frantically. In a minute, recess would be over and everyone would come back.

When they returned, she was ready. The first few boys and girls to come in looked at her questioningly, but she gazed steadily at the chalkboard, which she did not really see; at the posters on the wall, though they were nothing but a blur of bright colors. And nobody stopped to speak to her.

The rest of the morning passed. Mr. Mackenzie did not call upon Sal. Children gave reports. They sang. They planned a science experiment. Through it all, Sal sat unheeding. Most of the time, she was counting. Every time she got to sixty, it meant another minute was over. She did not look at Libby or at Elsje. Once she wondered if Elsje had told only

Libby about her cheating—or if she had told everyone. It was too terrible to think about.

Then class was dismissed.

Sal got to her feet even more slowly than usual. By the time she got to her locker, all but one or two of the girls had gone. She put on her coat, without talking to anyone. Then she went home.

Mother was at the stove making cream sauce when she came in. She sent a smile across the kitchen.

"Well, Sarah Jane, how was school?"

Until that moment, Sal had imagined that she would be able to pour out the whole story to Mother, but Elsje was right. She couldn't admit what she had done. Not even to her mother.

"Fine," she answered, looking away from that smile.

Mother's hand stilled on the mixing spoon.

"Just 'Fine'?" she began gently. "Is that all, honey?"

Sal became very busy undoing her coat button.

"It was fine," she repeated stubbornly.

All at once, her mother had somehow turned into a stranger who was going to poke and pry into the awful secret of all that had gone wrong that morning.

But Mother didn't pry. The sauce was ready and the rest of the family were waiting in the dining room.

"Get washed, dear. It's time to eat," she said quietly, and let Sally go.

Once, at the table, Dad challenged her with "So you weren't so 'different' after all, Sally?"

But when Sal only answered "No" and kept her head down, he suddenly started teasing Melinda instead.

She finished her lunch. She combed her hair, and was surprised to see that new, pretty Sally still there in the mirror. She put on her coat. She said good-by to Mother and gulped back a sudden rush of tears when her mother caught her by the shoulders and gave her an extra kiss before she let her go. Then she went back to school for the afternoon.

Nothing exciting happened. A few minutes before afternoon recess, it started to rain. Several children stayed in the room reading books or playing games. Sal looked thankfully at the streaming windowpanes and hid behind the book Libby had brought her that morning.

Mother and Dad will send me back to Allendale, she comforted herself as the class discussed the Antarctic; when I tell them I really want to go back, they'll send me.

But she knew it was an empty promise. Her parents had sounded so sure of themselves the day before. She would have to tell them why.

"Class dismissed," Mr. Mackenzie said at last—and it was over.

Once again, Sal stayed at her desk, letting the others get ahead of her. Libby sent her a quick, sorry glance, but Sal missed it. She was watching Elsje's straight back and the proud way she walked through the door. She was thinking that Elsje would never forget, never in a trillion years!

She must have told everyone, Sal thought bitterly. I was scared they'd stare at me because of my crutches. But they're all staring because they know I'm a cheater!

"Sally, would you stay for a moment, please. I'd like to talk with you."

"I . . . Yes, sir." Sal studied Mr. Mackenzie's face. She could see nothing there but friendliness. The last child went out of the room and the door closed.

The teacher came over and sat down on the desk beside hers.

"First of all," he said, "I want to say how sorry I am that you have had so difficult a day. I could have made it much easier for you if I had used my head."

Sal stared at him blankly.

"I forgot about the way we stand for the opening exercises," he reminded her. "I forgot to check beforehand to see whether you could handle the arithmetic drill. And, perhaps most important of all, I forgot about Elsje."

Sal's eyes were wide with disbelief.

"You mean, you KNOW about the arithmetic?" she quavered.

"Yes, I know about it." His face crinkled into a smile. "We teachers are smarter than we look. I knew right while it was happening. But it was too late to help you then, Sally. Tomorrow, why don't you get your sheet numbered ahead of time. I think that extra second per question is all you'll need. You got a couple of them, you know."

Sal nodded.

"That's fine then. Don't be afraid to leave blanks if you can't keep up."

"I didn't mean to cheat!" Sal burst out, so glad to be telling someone at last that the words tumbled over one another in their eagerness to be said. "I started to put down the numbers and then I was scared and—Well, it just sort of happened!"

"Being afraid makes things like that happen once in a while," he agreed.

He paused and gave Sal a long keen look. Then he continued quietly: "Elsje Jansen is the one who would really understand how you felt. If Libby hadn't been here last year to help her, I don't know what she would have done. You see, Elsje was even more frightened than you on her first day at school."

7

Piet's Sister

"ELSJE . . ." Sal repeated after him.

She was still so full of relief at having confessed about the arithmetic that, for a moment, Elsje's name meant nothing to her. Then, she remembered. The next minute, she found herself telling Mr. Mackenzie all about Elsje too.

"She never even tried to like me," she finished stormily. "Before she spoke one word to me, she was wishing I hadn't come here. Well, she should be happy because I'm going to get my mother and father to send me back to Allendale. I don't have to stay here!"

Her words sounded defiant and sure in the quiet classroom, but still deep inside Sally was that knowledge that they meant nothing. Her parents had planned too long and too carefully. They had brought her home to stay. Mr. Mackenzie seemed to know it too, for he made no answer to her talk of leaving. Instead he looked at her as though he were measuring her, as though he were making sure of something about her before he said anything more.

"Sally," he began, at last, his voice sounding very much like Dad's, "I'd like to tell you a story—a story about Elsje."

Sal ran her thumbnail back and forth over a little crack in her desk. There was nothing she wanted to know about Elsje.

"I don't blame you for feeling that Elsje is the one who

needs to show some understanding right now," Mr. Mackenzie went on, as though Sal had answered him. "But I'd like you to listen to the story anyway, and then see what you think. I am trusting you with this story because I know your father and mother and Melinda and Kent, and because I feel as though I know you even though we only met this morning."

Sal stopped poking at the crack but she kept her head lowered. She wished it were over, because nothing he could say was going to change her mind about Elsje Jansen.

"When you came through that door this morning and faced our class, you were frightened. Anyone would have been, some just a little, some a whole lot. But frightened as I know you were, Sal, your fear was nothing compared to Elsje's a little over a year ago.

"Her family had been in Canada only about six weeks. Just after they arrived, her brother Pieter became seriously ill. Her father and mother were so worried about him that they didn't have much time left over for helping Elsje to get adjusted to a strange land. Did you say something, Sal?"

"No," Sal said.

When Piet had come into the story, she had started to listen in spite of herself. Pieter Jansen was a stranger to her. But Kent had said "Nobody likes Piet!" and Sal wanted to know why.

Mr. Mackenzie went on. "As far as I have been able to learn, Elsje just stayed in the house most of that time. She didn't know any English and she was too shy to try to make friends with children she could not talk to nor understand. Then the Jansens were told that Elsje would have to start school the day after Labor Day.

"Her mother brought her as far as the door, but she was as

out of place as Elsje. She was shy and she must have had to leave Pieter alone to come with Elsje, because Mr. Jansen would already have gone to work. In any event, she whispered good-by at the door and hustled off. Elsje just stood there."

Mr. Mackenzie's voice grew suddenly husky. He stopped and cleared his throat.

"I have never seen any person look as terrified as that child did in that moment, Sal. She was dressed differently from the other girls, but it was her face that made us all catch our breath. She was very white. She looked as though she would be sick if anyone so much as took a step in her direction. None of us dared to stir. We might be sitting there yet if Libby hadn't arrived.

"You've met up with our Libby yourself so perhaps you can guess what happened next. She took one look at the new girl standing frozen in the doorway. She made a little noise like a mother hen noticing a chick in trouble. Then she marched over, gave Elsje that famous smile of hers, put her arm firmly around her waist and took her over to her own desk. In two seconds flat, Elsje had a chair next to Libby's and Libby was proudly practicing her first Dutch word."

Mr. Mackenzie cleared his throat again. Sal found she had to clear hers too.

"They've been 'best friends' ever since. Elsje has other friends by this time, but Libby is the one she counts on, the one she turns to when her mother and father don't understand Canadian ways or when they get too tied up with Piet's troubles. For a long time she has been sure that Libby was hers for keeps."

Mr. Mackenzie looked down at Sal's bright face, full of pity and warmth now. He smiled a little.

"Then," he said quietly, "you came."

Sal's eyes widened with the shock. Why, of course, this "Elsje" was the girl she had said she hated.

She took a deep breath.

"What did I do to her?" she asked, at last, in a small voice.

"Nothing on purpose," the teacher told her. "But, you see, Elsje knew, before she ever saw you, that you were handicapped. Couldn't that mean that you were going to need a lot of special attention, like Piet? What's more, she knew that you would be living just one block from Libby, while the Jansens live three blocks away. Perhaps—most worrying of all—she guessed that you would be frightened coming into a classroom full of strange children. Elsje has reason to remember how kind Libby is to anyone who is afraid. I don't think Elsje said all these things to herself, Sally, but I do think she might have been anxious about them down deep in some corner of her heart. Then, this morning, she walked in and found that she was right. Libby was being just as friendly to you as she had been to Elsje on that other first day. And she was afraid that she was going to lose her 'best friend.' "

Mr. Mackenzie had told his story well. Sal raised a sober face to the man who sat watching her.

"I don't know what to do about it," she said finally. "Libby won't be my friend now, anyway, so Elsje doesn't have to worry any more."

"Libby *will* be your friend," Mr. Mackenzie contradicted her. "That was probably what frightened Elsje the most. There is something special between you and Libby just as there was between Libby and Elsje. Libby is friendly with everyone, but she lights up like that for very few. You will have to be understanding. You will have to be patient. You will even have to be brave. But, someday, you will find that you have a new friend—and I hope that Elsje will discover that friendship can be shared. Enough of a lecture for today, Sally. Your mother will be thinking you got lost by the wayside."

That night, when Mother came in to say good night, Sal told her what she had done that morning. With Mother's arms around her, the words came easily and Sal could hardly believe that a few hours ago she had been certain it was too terrible to tell. She was going to go on about Elsje, but she found it was all mixed up in her head between Mr. Mackenzie's story and her memory of Elsje's stinging words. She was too tired to straighten it out. Besides, something told her that it was only the beginning of a story. She yawned and then sighed, a deep, quivering sigh full of all the hurt the day had brought to her.

"Hush now, Sarah Jane," Mother murmured softly. "It's all over. Hush and close your eyes."

Without another word, Sal slept.

Today will be different, she told herself as she set out for school on Tuesday morning. I will show them I want to be friends with them both.

She was there early, so she was at her desk when the two girls came down the aisle.

"Good morning," Sal said.

Elsje's eyebrows rose a little. Then she answered coolly for both of them.

"Good morning."

Sal said "Hi" that afternoon, and "Good morning" again on Wednesday, still hoping it would work. After that, she only spoke because Mr. Mackenzie was watching. Libby looked bothered each time. But it was always Elsje who answered, coolly and without a smile.

Sal went to Kent's room on Wednesday after school. He was crouched by his guinea-pig hutch feeding No-Tail and Squeak stalks of celery.

"Kent," she said, standing just inside the door, "why doesn't anybody like Piet Jansen?"

Kent dropped the celery. He stared at her.

"What do you care?"

"I just want to know, that's all. You said 'Nobody likes Piet.' Why not?"

"I'm not going to talk about it," Kent said, his eyes darkening.

Now it was Sally who stared.

"Why not? You started it! You said . . ."

"I don't care what I said!" Kent yelled at her, springing up and pushing past her. "I'm not going to say one more word about Piet Jansen, so don't ask me."

"But—" Sally began.

Her brother was gone.

The next morning, she sat at her desk, clutching her pencil, trying to shut out of her heart the snub Elsje had just given her. "Good morning" was such a simple thing to say, but every day it was growing harder. Now she was supposed to be writing another story, but she could not think about it. All at once, a door slammed. Everyone jumped, but Sal, partly because she had been lost in a world of her own and partly because of her cerebral palsy, leaped a good two inches higher than anybody else in the room. She knocked one crutch against the other. Her braces clanged against the metal legs of the desk. She said "Oh!" out loud, before she could stop herself, and her pencil flew from her hand and landed halfway up the aisle.

A boy brought it back to her. It was the brown-haired, brown-eyed boy who had given out the sheets of paper for the arithmetic test. As he handed her the pencil, he smiled.

"Thank you," Sal said.

She did not return his smile. She thought: Elsje must have told him about me by now.

She would not let herself believe in the friendly grin that had lighted up his brown eyes. Just the same, she listened until she learned his name—Jon Nordway. Why, he was the one Mindy had called a "darling little boy."

That night at supper Sal asked Dad to let her go back to Allendale.

Kent had been talking for several minutes before she could gather up enough courage to approach her father. She was not listening or she would have known that he was talking about her.

"Sal's the only one without a pet," he was arguing, "and I say she should have a dog." He then went down the list of animals the family already owned, as though the rest did not know it as well as he. "Mindy has Purrpuss. I have No-Tail and Squeak. Meg has that turtle, Fifty Cents. I still think that's a crazy name for a turtle."

"That's how big he is and how much he cost," Meg said calmly.

"Only Sal has nothing—and what she wants is a dog, isn't it, Sal?"

Sal did not answer and the rest of the Copelands laughed. It was no secret that Kent himself had wanted a dog for years.

He would have had a dog if a boy at school had not turned up with two guinea pigs in his pockets and offered to trade them for Kent's fountain pen. The guinea pigs had been alive and on the spot and the dog was still only in Kent's imagination, so he had come home with the two small animals. He had become fond of them, but he still yearned for a dog, and now Sal's coming had given him a good excuse for getting one.

"Sal, are you deaf?" he asked now. "I said, you'd like a dog, wouldn't you?"

Sal looked at him and shivered. She was terrified of dogs. She had never known one well, but at Allendale there had been a huge watchdog who was kept chained during the day. Terrible stories had been told after "Lights Out" about things Bruno would do to a burglar if he ever caught one. And one of the teachers had had a very old spaniel who snarled whenever a child came within earshot. No, she didn't want a dog. But she was not going to talk about it right now.

"Dad," she said, faltering in spite of herself, ignoring Kent completely, "I was wondering . . . I want to go back to Allendale."

"You've finished." Dad nodded at the other three children. "You are excused."

When they had gone, he reached out and took Sal's tightly clenched fist in his big hand.

"Sally, can you tell us what is wrong?" he asked.

Sal looked back at him helplessly. How could she? It was bigger than her quarrel with Elsje, she knew. It was something wrong with her. Maybe if she told him "I'm like Piet . . ."

She looked away from him, away from Mother, too, whose eyes were so full of love.

"There's nothing special wrong. I just don't like it here.

At school. I just thought maybe . . . you wouldn't care . . . if I went back."

Dad released her hand. Mother gave a quick little sigh.

Then Dad said, "But we do care, Sal. No, I'm sorry if you are not happy here, but you are a part of our family and we feel you belong with us. Maybe you will learn how to be happy if you try a little longer."

Sal did not cry. She felt as though she were shrinking, the way Alice had in Wonderland. Mother and Dad seemed huge and not at all real. Without saying anything more, Sal started to get herself up onto her crutches.

"You are excused," Dad told her gently, and she clumped out of the room.

On Friday morning, Mr. Mackenzie was watching Sally, so she said "Good morning," but she did not look up. Not once, during the day, did she try to make friends with anyone. She thought she had stopped caring. Sal Copeland was shutting herself away behind a high wall, where neither Kent's talk of her getting a dog nor Elsje's ignoring her could frighten or hurt her any longer.

8

I Want That Dog

THE NEXT DAY, Sal got her dog.

In the morning, Dad drove Mother, Sally and Meg to Toronto to see Dr. Eastman. Dr. Eastman was Sally's specialist. Their family doctor had referred them to him as soon as they had realized that Sal had cerebral palsy.

After he had checked her over, watched her walk and lifted her onto a table while he examined her to see she was "still working properly" as he put it, the doctor turned to find Meg standing at his elbow, her face one big question.

"What's the matter with her, do you know?" Meg asked him.

"Do please explain," Mother said. "I've done it before and I'll do it again but you do it so much better than I."

Dr. Eastman shook his head as though he did not believe that, but he sat down facing Meg and Sally.

"Your brain is like a motor," he told them. "Part of this motor makes you walk. Part of it makes you talk. Part of it makes you able to use your hands easily. Another part helps you to see, another to hear, and so on. If you are going to be able to walk and use your hands well, you have to have the motor part of your brain in good working order besides having well-built arms and legs."

"I walk just on legs," Meg remarked, not believing a word of it.

"Sure you do—just as a car runs on its wheels. But if the motor wasn't in the car too, or if the motor in the car was broken, than what would happen?"

Meg thought about it.

"It wouldn't go," she admitted.

Dr. Eastman smiled. "You're right. It wouldn't," he said. "And it's the same with the brain. Most babies are born with the motor part of their brain all ready to go. But once in a while a baby is born with part of its motor broken—or injured, in other words."

Sal's eyes were bright with excitement. So that was why children with cerebral palsy were handicapped in so many different ways!

"Do you fix the broken parts or do you buy new parts?" Meg had more questions ready.

"I wish we could buy new parts," Dr. Eastman said. "We can't fix the broken or injured parts, Meg, and there isn't any place where you can buy new brains. But sometimes we can get other parts of the brain to do the work of the injured or broken part. It's as though you had to fix your car motor by getting another motor and working with it and trying it over and over until it worked—not as well as the right motor would have, but well enough to get the car moving. You learned how to drive the motor part of your brain when you learned to walk. Now Sally has to do that too—but she has to start off with the wrong motor and work a lot harder at it and teach it how to work."

"Who is the teacher?" Meg asked, looking Sal over as though she expected to see some special little person peeking out of her ear.

"The therapists who give her treatment help," he answered, "but the person who does most of it is, as I said, Sally herself."

Sal stared at him, sure he was mixed up, but he only nodded, smiling.

"Yes, you. Every time you do something yourself, getting yourself dressed maybe" (Sal blushed, thinking back) "or walking across a room, or anything that means putting the brain to work for you, it gets more used to its new job and does it a bit better. Mind you, it takes years and years for it to learn. Brains aren't too brainy, I guess," he finished.

Sal was still thinking about what he had said when they were out in the car. She wished somebody had told her about it years ago, but maybe it wouldn't have seemed so simple then. Meg still had it muddled.

"Be careful, Daddy," she said, as Dad lifted Sal down the steps. "You might break her brains more."

Halfway home, they began to notice the kennels.

"BOXERS: PUPPIES FOR SALE," Dad read out. "And there is a cocker kennel. We might just buy that dog of yours this afternoon, Sally."

For once, Sal was paying attention, and she opened her mouth to tell him, once and for all, that she did not want a dog, when suddenly Meg squealed, "Oh, stop, Daddy, STOP! Look at the tiny white puppies!"

Dad slowed down. Behind a wire fence, set well back from the road, four balls of lively white fur were tumbling over each other in a spirited game of I'm the King of the Castle.

"What breed are they?" Mother wondered. "Oh, there's a sign. WEST HIGHLAND WHITE TERRIERS. They are sweet. Do you suppose they're for sale?"

"No time like the present for finding out." Dad swung the car into the driveway of the kennel. From inside the nearby house, a cheery voice called, "I'll be out in just a second. Make yourselves at home."

"Let's go look," Meg begged, her head already hanging out the window.

The Copelands piled out of the car just as a woman left the house and came to meet them, her hand out in welcome.

"Those pups lured us right in off the highway," Mother said, smiling warmly. "We're in the market for a dog just now . . ."

Sal drew a deep, protesting breath but it turned into a relieved sigh as the woman shook her head ruefully.

"I'm sorry, but they aren't for sale yet. In another month they'll be old enough. We keep some of our dogs to show and we like to be sure we don't lose a champion. I do have one dog for sale, but she's not a pup any longer. I'll show her to you, though."

"Oh, we'd want a pup . . ." Mother began, but the lady was off already back to the house. Sal studied Mother's face. She was safe. Mother had no intention of buying this dog.

The screen door slammed. Sal turned. And her eyes fixed on a bundle of shivering fur in the kennel-lady's arms.

"What's her name?" Meg asked, peering at the shaggy little dog.

"She has a fancy kennel name, but I've just been calling her Susie. You could give her any name you wanted. She's a bit timid with strangers yet, but she'd get over that in no time."

"No," Mother said, smiling and stretching out a hand to pat Susie's back, which was all she could see of her. "I think Sal wants a puppy."

But Sal took a sudden step forward. She had been staring at Susie ever since the woman had brought her out. One thing was certain—Susie was scared stiff. She was shaking, and she kept burrowing her head into the woman's arm as though she wanted to hide. Her tail was tucked under her and her coat was all rubbed up the wrong way.

Just then, the woman reached down and set her on her feet. Susie cowered before them, head hanging. She didn't run. She curled up as though she hoped somehow she would drop into the earth and disappear. Meg had turned back to the pups, but Sal leaned over as far as she could and looked at this small dog. Then, all at once, Susie lifted her shaggy face. Through the mat of tangled hair that almost covered it, Sal saw her brown eyes gleaming, begging someone to rescue her, saying that she knew all about what a queer lost feeling in your stomach felt like.

Sal drew a shaking breath. Then—"I want that dog," said Sarah Jane Copeland.

And, stunned by what she had said, she said it again, her voice wobbling wildly. "I want that dog right there, for mine!"

"Sally, what in the world," Mother started, but before she could say more, Dad announced, "That settles it. We'll take her."

Sal stood there, a little dazed, watching the arrangements being made. Mrs. Miller told the Copelands a great deal about Susie. She was already housebroken. She had a fine pedigree. Her kennel name was Roseneath Rosette.

Then they were back at the car. Dad helped Sally into the back seat.

"Here's your dog, Sal," he said, and placed Susie on the seat beside her.

At that moment, Sal understood what she had done. She wanted to dive to the other side of the car and yell: "No. I didn't mean it! Take her away!"

But Susie did not even look at her. She lay down on the seat with her nose plunged out of sight in the corner by the far door. The hump of her that she couldn't hide looked so miserable that Sal sat back and felt miserable along with her. The car swept out of the drive. They were bound for home—*and she had a dog.*

Before they had gone ten miles, Sal could not stand it any longer. Timidly, ready to jerk back if Susie so much as sneezed, she inched her way closer to the small lonely dog. Gently, her hand as light as a feather, she reached out and patted her. Susie lay still. Sal's touch grew surer, more comforting.

Susie didn't move away, although she was still shivering. At last, Sal cleared her throat and said huskily, "Don't be scared, Susie. Please, don't be scared."

When her mother glanced back at her ten minutes later, she was patting the shaggy little rump steadily and crooning, "Good girl . . . good little Susie. . . . Don't be scared. . . . I'll look after you."

Every so often, Sal caught the tip of Susie's ear flicking back just a little, as though she were hearing every single word. "There it goes again," she thought, her hand steadier, her voice soft as a spring wind. "She knows I'm talking to her."

In the front seat, Meg had fallen asleep. Her mother spoke very softly to her father.

"Blessings on you, Andrew," she said. "I think you were right. She's coming out of her shell already."

Sal wriggled over a little closer to Susie. Shyly, she moved her hand up to where the dog's head was turned into the corner of the seat cushion.

"Do you like to be scratched behind your ears?" she whispered to that one ear, flicking back at her. "All dogs in books like it."

Her fingers worked through the coarse coat till she could feel the short soft fur right next to the terrier's skin. Susie gave no signs of knowing her fingers were there, unless perhaps she trembled a little more. Sal scratched, and scratched—and went on scratching. At last, so slightly that Sal wondered if she might be imagining it, Susie moved her head. She pressed closer to the hand that felt so good, so consoling, just behind her ear.

Deep in the warm fur, Sal's fingers kept up their scratching, and above the little dog's head her voice still crooned. But now Sal's voice was breathless with excitement, and Susie was not the only one who trembled.

Then, unbelievably, Susie twisted her nose out of the crack between cushion and door, and a wet ribbon of tongue darted out for one hurried lick at Sal's hand. The hand was still. Sal could not move it. Susie, too, seemed frozen into a statue of a small wary dog, taken aback by her own daring. But then, she turned her body even further around with a rough little thud and began to sniff at Sal's fingers.

She's stopped trembling, Sal thought, dazed. She's stopped trembling. She's beginning to like me.

She looked out through the window at the October sky ablaze with blue and at the glowing maples. Everything seemed so bright, brighter than ever before, even at noon, as though someone had doubled the sunlight. The loveliness of it made her eyes sting, but although she blinked, the blurred, shining beauty did not vanish nor dim to an ordinary day.

Sal sat blinking and wondering why she was almost crying when, for once, she was happy clear down to her toes. Then she felt the rough, doggy tongue begin licking away at her hand with steady devotion.

As they neared Riverside, Meg wakened and, at once, her tousled head popped up over the front seat. For several seconds, she simply gazed at Susie, who went right on washing Sal's fingers as though nobody were watching.

"That's your dog, isn't it, Sally?" she said, at last.

"Yes, she is," Sal said, almost whispering lest she break the spell in the back seat.

"Is she Kent's dog too?"

"No," Sal said, suddenly looking at Meg instead of at Susie. "She's mine."

"Yours for keeps?" Meg sounded deeply impressed.

Then Sal remembered how short a time she had known this little dog—less than two hours—and how afraid she had been when they had turned in at the kennel, and she was amazed at the rush of love in her heart.

"Yes, Meggy," she said firmly. "Mine for keeps."

9
Sally's Shadow

THAT WEEKEND was full of surprises.

First, Sal was so worried about Susie that she got herself out of the car without waiting for anyone to help her. She reached the curb safely, talking soothingly over her shoulder to the little dog the whole time. Then, all at once, there was nothing to hold on to, and she would have landed on her nose on the grass if Dad had not caught her neatly. Calmly, he handed her her crutches. Then he broke down and shot her a proud smile.

"Way to go, Sarah Jane," he said.

Between them, they got Susie into the house. Mother was slow coming in from the car. By the time she arrived, Susie was deposited on Sal's bed with both Sal and Meg crooning over her.

Mother looked firm.

"She can't sleep in here, girls," she told them.

The girls did not answer. They smiled briefly at her and went on talking to Susie.

"She'll have to sleep in the cellar," Mother said, "or maybe the back hall. We'll fix a nice box for her."

Neither Sally nor Meg bothered to argue. Mother hadn't made up her mind. Wait till they had Kent and Melinda, maybe even Dad, on their side.

Kent and Melinda came home together that day. Meg,

nearly bursting with importance, was waiting for them at the door.

"Guess what?"

"What?" countered Melinda, and Kent, slinging his library books onto the hall table, tried to push past her.

But Meg was not going to be robbed of her big moment.

"Sally's got a dog!" she shouted.

Mindy grabbed her. Kent whooped with excitement. But Meg shushed them sternly. "This dog is SCARED!" she told them, her own voice rising to a bellow. Her brother and sister did not wait to hear more. They were off to see for themselves.

As they went into the bedroom, they were quiet suddenly. The small white dog on the bed looked at them once, quivered all over, and turned back to her mistress.

"Oh, she's darling," Melinda glowed. Her dark hair was hanging down and, framed in it, her eager face seemed all alight as she gazed at Susie.

Kent, squatting down beside her, gazed just as hard, but differently. He had been wanting a dog for such a long time. Their other house had faced on a busy highway. The yard had been small and unfenced. Dad had made sense when he had said "no dog." And then, there had come No-Tail and Squeak. But now, things had changed. Studying Susie, Kent knew that, when he had campaigned for a dog for Sal, he had hoped all along that the dog would really be his when it arrived. His hope began to die as he saw the look on Sal's face. Still, Susie *was* a dog. His smile broke out as brightly as Mindy's.

"She's swell!" he whispered.

They almost came to blows though over her name. Sal had not once stopped to think what to call the little dog. Somehow, she had just been Susie. Kent was indignant. "Susie" was no name for a thoroughbred, he raged. Mindy said dreamily, "No, Sal. Susie isn't Scottish enough. It had better be Tammy. Good girl, Tammy." And she patted Susie's flattened ears.

Sal looked at them both, Kent scarlet with anger, Mindy paying no attention to either of them. Mindy was the strongest, she knew. There was nothing she could do against Mindy.

Then Dad walked in, with Meg on his shoulder. Kent whirled to meet him, spilling out the story. Mindy looked up calmly. "See, she knows her name's Tammy already," she announced.

"What *are* you going to name your dog, Sal?" Dad asked pleasantly.

There was no ducking the question. He had given it to her. Susie gave her hand one quick lick. Sal shut her eyes to all faces but Dad's. In the same voice she had used for saying "I want that dog!"—the same frantic, once-and-for-all, wobbly voice—she said:

"Her name's Susie. I can't help it. Susie's just her name."

Kent kicked the bedpost. Melinda looked hurt. But nobody argued. Maybe there was something to be said for standing up for your rights.

"Come on, son," Dad said. "How about helping me knock together a bed for this dog?"

For a moment, Kent glared. Then he grinned instead.

"Okay," he growled. "I guess I'll get used to Susie. . . . Do you *have* to come everywhere *we* go, Tag-along?"

Meg, trotting out of the room right at his heels, nodded. Mindy and Sal laughed together and the hurt between them disappeared.

After supper, Dad and Kent brought the dog's new bed up to Sally's and Meg's room. It was a three-sided box which stood off the ground on four square blocks. All they had to do was fold an old quilt and lay it inside the box to make a perfect bed. It just fit between the girls' beds, and it was easy for Susie to get into herself.

Just before Sal climbed into bed, she settled Susie into hers. Mother, who had come in to cover Meg and say a whispered good-night, gave Sal a kiss and Susie a pat, and tiptoed out of the room. All at once, Susie whimpered in the darkness. Sally rolled over to the edge of her bed and patted the little dog.

"Don't, Susie," she begged, stroking the rough coat and feeling that tongue again licking at her hand. "I'm right here."

But the moment she took her hand away, Susie, used to a kennel full of other dogs, began to whimper again—little lonely sounds that hurt Sal. Then she got down out of her box and put her front paws up on the side of Sally's bed. Sal was so thrilled she couldn't even speak. She braced herself as best she could and tugged at Susie, trying to help her up on the bed beside her. She could not do it. She felt herself slipping and had to let go. Susie padded away in the darkness and, for a minute, Sal came close to crying too. She could hear the little dog climbing back into the box, turning around and around as though she were searching for something. But she didn't lie down. Sal heard her panting. All at once, there was a scrabble of paws and she jumped and landed right beside Sally's chest.

"Oh, you smart thing," Sal gasped. "You're the smartest dog that ever was!"

Susie explored the length of the bed, snuffling around Sal's toes until Sal thought she would giggle loud enough to wake Meg. Finally, the dog turned around a couple of times and plunked herself down against Sal's legs with a tired but contented little sigh.

Sal moved her legs a little so she could feel the small sturdy body nestled against them.

"My, Mother would be mad!" she thought. Hidden in the night, she could feel her face stretching into an enormous smile of satisfaction.

The next day, where Sal went Susie followed. She watched while Sal sat drying dishes for Mother. She lay on the bed at Sal's side while Sal read *The Expandable Browns.* Even when Sally only had to go to the bathroom, the little dog refused to be left behind. On Sunday morning, when the family went to church, Sal felt like a deserter. All through the service, she worried. When they got home, however, there was Susie, safe and sound, right inside the door, her tail wagging furiously.

"Hello, Sally's shadow!" Kent greeted her.

Sal beamed at him as she bent to tell her dog, Yes, it was all right, they were really home!

School was different on Monday. Sal was full of thoughts of Susie. How strange it was that she never barked—only growled fiercely if she thought someone was going to hurt Sal. How funny it was to be wakened in the morning by a real live animal walking up the bed to peer at her through tangly bangs and sniff "Hello"! How lovely it was to feel Kent and Melinda watching, as Susie trotted along everywhere at her heels! She was so busy with these thoughts that she did not even notice Elsje and Libby when they came down the aisle to their seats.

Maybe Elsje had come to expect that small "Good morning" from Sal and missed it. Or maybe it was the look on Sal's face—a bright, dreaming look that turned her into quite a different girl from the one who had faced up to Elsje with such determination every day for a week. Whichever it was, Elsje Jansen paused for a moment and stared at her. Sal did not even see her pause. If she had, she might have been startled by something in Elsje's eyes, almost a question.

But if Elsje was asking herself anything, Sal was too happy to notice. A moment later, Elsje had turned away.

After school, Sal did not dawdle. She wanted to get home to Susie too badly. She hurried out and got her coat on with all the other girls. Once, glancing up, her eyes met Libby's, and loneliness washed over her like a wave. "Susie's waiting for me," she reminded herself then. She sped out the door and swung along the sidewalk as fast as her crutches would carry her. She did not let herself think of the other girls again.

Libby Reeves had seen the sudden look of aloneness on Sally's face. She did not speak of it to Elsje. She knew that Elsje had seen it too.

Just before supper that night, Sal and Melinda had another battle. On Saturday and Sunday Mother had fed Susie, although it was the custom in the Copeland family for the owner to take care of his or her own pet. No one had said anything about it until Melinda announced, too sweetly, "From now on, Sal, I'll feed Susie for you. I don't mind doing it."

Sal flushed.

"I want to feed her myself," she said, her voice uncertain.

Melinda was so reasonable, so sure of herself, just as she had been when she christened Susie "Tammy."

"But you can't, honey," she cooed. "How would you get the bowls down on the floor without spilling them or falling over yourself?"

Sal stood by, seething helplessly, as Mindy began to get out dog biscuits and ground beef. But Melinda brought about her own downfall.

"I'm feeding Susie for Sal from now on," she trilled at Dad as he walked down the hall.

Dad was in the kitchen in two strides.

"Did you ask her to do your job, Sal?" he asked.

"No!" Sal burst out, glaring at her sister.

"Then I suggest you leave Sally's work for Sally to do," Dad ordered with a bite in his voice that made Melinda put down the bowl in her hand as though it were red-hot.

Through with pretending to be sweet, Mindy glared back at Sal.

"But, Dad, she *can't* . . ." she started.

It appeared Sal could. Dad had made a cart on wheels for just that purpose. He showed Sal how to work it. When the food was mixed and the water dish filled, Sal had only to set them on the tray and push the cart across the kitchen. Then, bracing the cart against the wall and holding her breath, she could use one hand to lift the bowls down to the floor, one at a time. If she only half-filled the bowl with water and if she held her breath just so, it worked.

"I CAN do it, Susie," she crowed.

Tuesday came and went. By Wednesday morning, every child in Sal's class had noticed the difference in her. As she bent over her books, a smile curving her lips, they watched her uneasily. Nothing nice had happened to her, as far as they knew, and yet, she did not seem to care any longer whether they spoke to her or left her alone.

Sal did care. Only Susie knew how she sometimes cried out in her sleep, dreaming about it. "Poor Piet!" Susie had heard her say once in the darkness, and not once but many times, she had sobbed, "I didn't mean to, Elsje, I didn't mean to!"

Mornings now brought Susie herself, though, chasing away the bad dreams, jumping all over Sal, asking for a game of tag. Thoughts of the little dog stayed with Sally all day long, helping her to push back the thought that nobody liked her at school.

Elsje Jansen tried not to look, but more and more often her puzzled gaze was drawn across the aisle to the bright face of the girl she would not befriend.

10

Halloween

WHEN SALLY COPELAND clumped into school on Friday morning, she positively glowed. No longer was she just dreamy. She was sparkling with excitement. Elsje turned sharply on Libby.

"Look at her," she said tersely. "What has happened to her?"

Libby's answer came very softly.

"I don't know, but somebody must have been awfully nice to her."

Elsje banged her arithmetic book open and began to study without another word.

Sal was remembering her "Place." Yesterday, after school, she had found it. The other three Copeland children had Places—special nooks where they could go when they did not want to be disturbed by anyone for any reason. Kent had a tree house. Melinda locked herself in her room. Meg climbed in the cupboard with the vacuum cleaner. Now Sal had the best Place of all.

Susie had really discovered it. They had been rambling around the big yard together when, all at once, the little dog had vanished. Sal had called. No Susie. She had circled tree trunks and looked around the corner of the house. No Susie. The only other spot where she might be hiding seemed to be behind a huge bush in the fence corner. Sal had squeezed

close to the fence, pushing aside a tangle of leaves and branches. And there was the Place!

The fence did not make a neat corner at all. Instead, it right-angled into a small, extra square of grass. Later on, Dad had explained that the people who had first owned the Copeland house had owned a great deal of property. In selling off the lots, either this bit had been overlooked or somebody had felt about it the same way Sal did and had kept it on purpose. It was about ten feet long and a little less in width. The fence rose around it on three sides and the barberry bush barred its entrance. There was nothing there but a stretch of scrubby lawn, but in the late afternoon, the sunlight had fallen between the fence boards and laid long slivers of golden light across it. And there, in the middle, had sat a small white dog, looking up at her as though to say, "Well, how do you like it?"

Sal tried hard to concentrate on fractions, but she kept thinking instead of how amazed the family had been when she had dragged them out to see her find. They had given her all sorts of things to put in it—an old wooden box to keep things in, an extra captain's chair, a stool, a ground sheet and a worn Indian blanket. Dad was going to squeeze himself in and put some rope handles and a bar on the fence so that Sal would be able to get herself up and down without any help.

Then, after supper, they had carved the jack-o'-lanterns. Sal looked around the classroom. There were witches and ghosts and pumpkins looking down at her from every window. And last night, for the first time in her life, she had carved a pumpkin head of her own. She was sure it would be a mess, and Mindy had, of course, offered to do it for her. But Dad had insisted that she do it herself. When it was done and she sat, her face hot, her hair mussed and pumpkin seeds up to her elbows, she knew that she had never seen such a wonderful jack-o'-lantern! One eye was much bigger than the other and the nose ran into the mouth, but the smile was wide and the mistakes just made him "interesting."

If you went by that, Meg's was even more "interesting"—for she would only give him one eye no matter what anyone said. Kent held his down for Susie to admire and she backed off, trying to pretend by growling ferociously that she wasn't scared out of her wits.

That afternoon, Mr. Mackenzie told them spooky stories

until Sal could feel the hair standing up on her head, just as she had read it did in books. Then he passed around apples and Halloween cookies.

Even the few arithmetic problems they did were special ones: "If a ghost-and-a-half met a goblin-and-a-half and they all turned into witches, how many witches would there be?"

Before supper, Kent and Melinda dressed up in their costumes.

Melinda was going to a masquerade as a pirate. Dad's rubber boots, a huge scarlet sash and a black patch over one eye made her look swashbuckling and dangerous indeed. As a last touch Mother had found two brass curtain rings and tied them onto her ears with thread.

Kent was disguised as an artist. He had thought of it himself. He wore a beret of Mindy's and an old smock of Mother's all over which he had splashed different colors of poster paint. He had a thick sketch pad and some charcoal and he planned to do a portrait of anyone who gave him something extra good. He was taking a huge shopping bag in which to "lug home the loot."

Sally couldn't remember spending Halloween at home before. She had been so little when she went away to Allendale and she had only come home for the two holidays each year, once at Christmas and once in the summer. At Allendale they had always had a big party for the children, but there was nothing like the feeling she had as she went out in the darkening yard and saw the four jack-o'-lanterns grinning through the wide front windows. Nor had there been anything like the excitement of watching Melinda and Kent turning into two entirely different people right before her eyes.

Just inside the front door, on a chair, stood a basket of polished apples, and beside it, bags of multicolored jelly-beans and jujubes, gumdrops and fat caramels. Before supper was finished the doorbell rang with a loud, long peal. Sal choked on her dessert and Meg swung her spoon, splattering pear juice far and wide.

"Is it Halloween NOW?" she demanded, her eyes round as saucers.

"It sure is!" Kent shouted. "Come on!"

Dessert forgotten, the whole family trooped to the door. Outside four boys waited, one dressed as a skeleton. Meg "Oo-oo-ed" at the sight of him. Kent knew all the others in spite of their costumes, but the skeleton had him stumped.

"You're Mark? Victor? Sammy?" Kent tried, peering at what little could be seen of the boy beneath the bones. They were painted in white on a black suit that covered him from head to heel.

Each time the skeleton denied the charge, answering first in the voice of a little old lady, then a small boy, then a giggly girl.

All at once, Kent cried, "I know! You're Rusty Sardis! Your Dad painted those bones on you. He's a doctor!"

"Rusty!" squeaked the skeleton. "Who's he? Never heard of him!"

Kent danced around, knowing he'd guessed right. A couple of hobos turned in at the end of the walk and Mindy gasped and hurried off to get the last couple of things she needed before she went off to her party.

Mother looked at Sal.

"I wish you were going, dear," she said, gently. "If Mindy hadn't been going to this masquerade . . ."

"I like it staying home," Sal answered quickly.

She got an apple out, ready to give to the next comer. She honestly didn't know whether she wished she were going out or not. It looked like fun, but frightening too, unless of course you had a friend.

Then, she was too busy to wonder. Meg would just get the door closed, when the bell would jangle again. Such weird and wonderful people as they found on the doorstep! Everyone from old Mr. Menzies next door, pretending to be Santa Claus come early, to children who looked younger than Meg, holding up bags as big as themselves, while their mothers waited in the shadows behind them.

At last, Mother came for Meg.

"Time for bed, little one," she said firmly.

Meg gave her a "What-on-earth-are-you-talking-about?" look.

"But it's still Halloween—isn't it, Sal?" she protested.

"One more then," Mother gave in.

The bell rang as though on cue. Meg rushed to fling it open. Libby and Elsje were standing on the step.

Elsje was disguised as a little old witch and she would have fooled anyone, but it was impossible to hide Libby under any costume. Her glasses, her freckles, her long skinniness and her smile showed through even though she wore a big red rubber nose and a clown suit patched all over in different colors as gay as any real clown's ever was.

"Trick or treat," Libby said weakly. "Shell out."

Sal, her hand shaking, reached for some gumdrops. They

slipped through her fingers, which had gone suddenly stiff, and she had to pick them up again. Her face flamed. Mother's voice, warm with interest, sounded from behind her.

"This clown and witch look about your size, Sal," she said. "Do you know who they are?"

"It's Libby," Sal heard herself saying hoarsely, "and Elsje. They're in my class."

She put the gumdrops into the paper bag Libby was holding open for her. She listened to them land, bumping loudly on the bottom of the bag. Then, the witch spoke:

"Do you not go out then on this Halloween?" she asked, as though the question were jolted out of her.

Sal answered, her voice as strained as Elsje's, "No. I—I'm staying home to help."

But Mother did not leave it at that.

"Sally's brother and sister went out with other friends," she remarked, her voice friendly and almost unconcerned. "Sal has never been out on Halloween, but maybe next year, she will know someone . . ."

Then, even Mother's voice trailed away as though she had just seen the way Sally was staring at the step and looking small and hunched between her crutches.

"Last year," Elsje said, her speech broken and harsh, "I went out for the first time on this Halloween. . . . I went with Libby. It is fun to go. You . . ." She stopped for a moment, looking at Sal out of her funny witch's face. Then she stepped into the hall with one swift motion and there finished what she had to say. ". . . You can come out now with Libby and me. We will take you."

Sal backed up, her eyes like a startled deer's.

"But—" she gasped— "But—I haven't got a costume!"

"Oh, I have an easy one for you," Libby cried, crowding in behind Elsje, gladness written all over her freckled face. "If your mother has an old sheet and some string . . ."

"Andrew," Mother called, "come and help Meg with the door."

She ran off down the hall, her skirts flying. Libby took Sal in from head to toe.

"If she could sit down," she said thoughtfully, as though Sally weren't there.

Sal felt as though she weren't, as though it were all happening to somebody in a dream. But Elsje couldn't be part of a dream. Not this Elsje. Still in her witch's tall hat, she dumped the apples and candies off the chair and dragged it over.

"Sit down," she commanded.

Sal sat.

In ten minutes, they had turned her into a ghost. The sheet had been draped over her and gathered in around her neck with the string. Mother, under Libby's direction, carefully snipped out eyes, nose and mouth while Sal, from inside the sheet, kept warning them not to stab her. Then they simply lifted her to her feet and trimmed the sheet off so that it came to about six inches above her ankles. Under the loose folds, she could move her crutches freely, and yet, when they led her to the hall mirror, she looked so ghostly she scared herself. Dad opened the door for her, Mother gave Libby an extra bag for her candy, and the three of them were off!

Never in all her life was Sally Copeland to forget that first Halloween. There was a moon peering down at them mysteriously through the tall black branches of trees. You could smell the smoke of bonfires still drifting in the cold, sweet air.

Almost every window had a jack-o'-lantern grinning or frowning crookedly out at them and, all evening, they passed gypsies and tramps, dancing girls and goblins abroad in the darkness. To Sal's delight they met Kent and his friends—and Kent didn't recognize her.

At first, no one said much. It was difficult to think of words. But soon Libby began to chatter happily, telling them all about the people who lived in the houses they visited.

"Old Lady Tracey always makes fudge for me because I cut her lawn in the summer. She puts nuts in it. Look, Jimmy Sacco's mother has a pumpkin up for him even though they just moved in here this afternoon. You'd think she'd be resting. She has arthritis or something. . . ."

It was not till they were almost home again that Sal mustered the courage to stop dead in the middle of the sidewalk and face Elsje.

"I'm sorry," she blurted—"about that arithmetic, I mean. I didn't tell Mr. Mackenzie, but he already knew. I didn't mean to do it. I just didn't know what to do—that first day."

She felt a lump crowding into her throat and her words stumbled. For a long moment, there was silence. Then Elsje muttered awkwardly:

"It is hard. To be new is hard. I . . . We shall forget it."

"Yeah," Libby burst in, her voice singing with relief. "Let's all of us forget it. Hey, let's save some of our candy and stuff and have a sort of picnic tomorrow."

"You could come to my house," Sal said eagerly. "I mean . . . There's this special Place, where Susie and I go to get away from Meg."

They had reached the Copelands' front door. The small ghost, whose face had slipped sideways so one eye was over her ear and she had only half a mouth to speak through, stood waiting, her heart thumping painfully. Under the lamplight, the clown and the witch looked at each other. Libby waited, not speaking. Once again, it was up to Elsje.

"Okay," said Elsje, sounding very Canadian and not a little shy. "Okay, Sal. We will come here."

"Hey, let's ring the doorbell and surprise your mother," suggested Libby.

They lined up, giggling. Then, with joy so huge inside her she was practically breaking in two, Sal reached out and pushed the bell.

11

The Wonderful, Horrible Day

"MEGGY. . . .MEG!"

Meg slept soundly on, her knees drawn under her, her bottom sticking up in the air.

"MEG, WAKE UP!"

"Go away!" Meg ordered crossly in her sleep.

"It's all right, Sal. I'm here," said Mother softly, coming into the room.

"How did you know I wanted you?" Sal asked as her mother started to help her into her braces.

"You said last night 'Tomorrow is going to be a wonderful day!' so I thought you'd be wanting to get started on it," Mother smiled.

"Wonderful, wonderful, wonderful! Did you hear that, Susie?" Sal sang under her breath as she pulled on her clothes. Susie lifted one ear politely.

"Be quiet, all of you. I'm SLEEPING!" Meg said clearly.

Sal laughed and reached for her crutches. She felt giddy with happiness. Libby and Elsje were coming after lunch and, for the first time since she had come home, she had beaten Meg getting dressed.

She gulped down her breakfast and hurried out to inspect her Place. Everything was ready. Dad and Kent had had trouble getting some things in past the barberry bush, but now they looked as though they had always been there—the old wooden box with the hinged lid which she called her "treasure chest," the captain's chair, and the low stool. Inside the chest were blankets and plastic-covered cushions. Now all she needed was a set of shelves for books, she thought, and maybe a roof over one end for rainy days, and . . .

"Sall-ee!"

A thudding of small feet interrupted Sal's dreams. Meg, breathless, popped into the Place like a jack-in-the-box.

"You're wanted on the telephone!" she announced.

"Me!"

"Yes. HURRY!"

Sal hurried. This really was a wonderful day, she thought, as she hurtled up the garden on her crutches. Nobody had ever called her on the telephone before. By the time she reached the house, she was as out of breath as Meg. Mother held out the receiver.

"Hello," panted Sal.

"Hi," said a voice.

Sal jumped a foot. She had not been ready for that voice speaking right into her ear.

"It's me, Libby," the voice went on, when Sal didn't say anything.

"Oh, hello," Sal said. The voice did not sound like Libby at all.

"Sal, I'm sorry, but my mother won't let me go out today. I caught a terrible cold last night. I guess you can tell by my voice. Anyway, my throat is sore and Mother says I have to stay in bed today."

"Oh," Sal said. That at least explained why Libby sounded so queer.

"I'm sorry, Sal."

"Yes," said Sal.

"Well, I'll see you at school on Monday, I guess."

"I hope you feel better," Sal got out at last.

"Oh, I will," croaked Libby. "Well . . . 'By."

"Good-by."

Sal hung up. Mother, Meg and Susie stood in a row, looking at her with sympathy.

"Was that Libby?" Mother asked. "She must have a dreadful cold."

At that, Sal burst into tears.

"It can't be THAT bad!" she sobbed noisily. "She could have come if she'd really wanted to. I hope she has a *terrible* cold! Her mother is just *mean,* that's all!"

"Sally, that's enough," Mother said sharply.

But Sal wasn't through. She grabbed the crutch nearest her and swung it savagely at the telephone table. The crutch tip caught in the telephone cord and jerked the phone to the floor with a terrific crash that sent Susie scuttling across the room, her tail between her legs.

"Oh, this is a *horrible* day!" Sal wailed. "I don't know what I'm going to do!"

"Well, I know what you're going to do," Mother told her, coldly. "You're going to stop making all that racket, and you're going to get up off your fanny and you're going to spend the morning cleaning up the mess in your bedroom."

"But—but—Mother," Sal stammered.

"But nothing," her mother retorted. "You seem to have a grudge against the world. You might as well count me in. Now, move!"

Sal spent the next hour furiously throwing things into place in her room, only to have Mother come in and insist that everything be taken out again and straightened and put away properly. As she worked, she kept telling herself, and anybody else who cared to listen, how much she hated everybody.

"Families are awful!" she declared once.

Kent went by, whistling. "You ought to know. You're part of one," he called in at her.

Lunch was a stormy meal. Meg spilled the milk. Dad came in tired and in no mood to listen to complaints. Since Sal and Mindy, who had also been sentenced to a morning of housecleaning, had nothing pleasant to say, he told them to keep quiet and eat.

It was a very silent family. Once Sal remembered how joyfully she had started the day, and she nearly wept in front of them all.

In the middle of their dessert, the doorbell rang.

"It's Mary Ellen," Mindy said, starting up.

"Sit down," Dad thundered.

"Oh, drat!" Mindy muttered, but she sank back onto her chair and managed to ask fairly civilly, "May I, please, be excused to answer the door?"

"Sure," Dad said maddeningly. "By all means. Don't keep the lady waiting."

Mindy dashed off, but she was back almost immediately.

"It's not Mary Ellen," she said. "It's someone for Sal."

Nobody was more surprised than Sally.

"Well, aren't you going to see who it is?" Dad asked, grinning at the stunned look on her face.

Sal scrambled up as fast as she could with everyone helping her. Down the hall she and Susie sped, moving faster than Susie ever remembered going before. The door was still open. There on the doorstep, smiling a little uncertainly, stood Elsje.

"Hi," she said. "I—Libby is sick. But I came. I brought with me Willem."

Susie growled low in her throat and Sal looked down. Willem was a long brown dachshund, sitting sedately by Elsje's foot.

"Well, gee," Sal gulped, her eyes suddenly shining like stars, "come on in. Come in, Elsje—and Willem too!"

Elsje stopped looking so terribly shy.

"Willem, *volg my,*" she ordered and walked in. Willem trotted obediently at her heel.

"No, Susie, NO!" Sal yelled.

Brave as a lion, for once, Susie was stalking toward this strange dog, roaring terrible threats at him as she came.

"It will be all right," Elsje said calmly. "Willem knows his manners. Let us watch them and see."

The Copelands, who had started to hasten to the rescue, stood back. Willem, who had sat down the moment Elsje stood still, now looked at Susie with interest, but with no sign of alarm. Susie kept coming, talking every step of the way about how some dogs had their nerve just walking into other dogs' houses and murder was none too good for such animals! When the enemy simply sat there, however, with his head cocked and his gaze warm with friendly curiosity, she paused. Puzzled, she looked up to Sal for help.

"Silly dog!" Sal scolded, sounding just like her mother. "Leave him alone. He's your friend. See, Elsje's my friend."

She put out her hand and touched Elsje's shoulder. Susie did not know what to do. She took one more step toward Willem, gave one more half-hearted growl and then sniffed at him. Willem sniffed back. Susie circled him, looking him over for concealed weapons. Finally Elsje murmured something softly to Willem, and he rose and inspected Susie in turn.

"Aw, I thought they'd fight!" Meg said, openly disappointed.

Sal looked down at the two dogs, her eyes startled. Why, less than a month ago, she had been afraid of dogs that growled, let alone dogs that fought. Yet here she had stood, telling Susie off, ready to shove the two of them apart with one of her crutches if she had to—and she had never stopped to think about being scared.

"Come on," she said quickly, blushing because all at once she felt proud of herself, "let's go, Elsje."

"Go where?" demanded Meg, planting herself right in front of Sally.

"Where you can't come with us, Margaret Ann," Sal retorted.

She moved her crutch forward and pretended she was going to put the tip of it down on Meg's toe. Meg had to jump back. She put her hands on her hips and scowled up at her big sister.

"Who wants to go with you anyhow?" she stuttered, jumping back again as Sal's crutch came too close for comfort. "But I'm not too little, so there. I'm a BIG girl."

Dad plucked her up from behind, holding her by the waist.

"Oh, you're enormous!" he said solemnly, flipping her over in the air. "You're tremendous! You're gigantic! You're so immense I can't even get you off the ground!"

He flipped her over again and Meg squealed with rapture.

Sal started for the door, but she had to stop and wait. Elsje was not following her. She was standing very still, watching Dad and Meg. Sal was going to tell her to hurry, but then she saw a queer look on Elsje's face. It was like the look that had been on Kent's face when he had first seen her with Susie. Before Sal could figure it out, though, Elsje swung around, her brown braids flying.

"Where is this Place you spoke of?" she asked.

"I'll show you," Sal said.

Her heart was filled with doubts as she led the way through the yard. Now that she thought about it, she really did not know Elsje at all. Maybe she just wasn't the kind of girl who liked special Places. She could so easily think it was too small or too empty and bare, or even plain silly.

Susie bounded around the barberry bush and disappeared. Sal took a deep breath, said a small prayer, and followed. Close behind her, Elsje and Willem found their way over the rough roots and through the tangle of branches. Then, they were there.

"Oh!" Elsje said.

It was enough. Sal looked at her excited face and sighed with relief. All at once, she saw it all with new eyes herself—the four tall sides closing them in like a private fortress, the early afternoon sunlight coming down to them in a long shaft as though they stood at the bottom of a well of light, the treasure chest, a book she had left open on the grass, the captain's chair holding out welcoming arms . . .

"It's kind of bare . . ." she began, watching Elsje closely.

"No, no," Elsje protested. "You do not want it to be just more garden. It is right like this. Libby will like it so much!"

Sal moved forward, clutched one of the handgrips Dad had put up on the fence for her, let go of her crutches and lowered herself onto the grass. Under her directions, Elsje delved into the treasure chest and brought out a blanket for them to sit on and some sandbag cushions. Her eyebrows rose as she felt how heavy they were. Sal laughed and explained.

"They keep me from slipping. I prop myself up with them. It's hard for me to sit on the ground like this because my body stiffens and I straighten out unless something is holding me. Watch."

She stuffed one of the brightly covered sandbags beneath her bent-up knees and placed others on each side of her. She had seated herself in a special spot she had found, where her heels were also propped against a grassy stone. Elsje watched with interest. Sal felt a bit queer under her frank gaze, but Elsje only nodded her head at the finish and got out a couple of cushions for herself.

"What's the password to this Kingdom-Behind-the-Barberry-Bush?"

Neither girl had heard anyone coming and both of them jumped at Mother's voice. Then Sal giggled. Mother's arm had appeared, and there was a cooky tin clutched in her hand. The rest of Mother stayed where it was.

"Hurry up," the voice said. "It's heavy."

Elsje sprang up and took the tin.

"Thanks," the voice said, going away. "You can keep the tin out here in your treasure chest. I have lots of others."

Inside were half a dozen fudge brownies. Susie, who had been showing Willem over the Place inch by inch, raised her head and sniffed the air. Without begging her guest's pardon, she deserted him and headed for the girls. Suddenly devoted, she nuzzled close to Sal, peering up through tousled bangs at the luscious square which was disappearing rapidly into Sally's mouth. "Aw, come on. I'm hungry too!" said her sniffing nose and her pleading eyes.

With a gurgle of laughter, Sal relented and broke off a bite for her. Then she looked up and saw Willem. He had tagged along, but he was now sitting neatly in front of Elsje, his gaze just as pleading, but much more polite. Not one undignified sniff showed how his mouth watered. He got an even bigger bite than Susie had been given.

"How did you ever teach him to be so good?" Sal asked, full of admiration. "Or does that kind of dog just naturally have good manners?"

"Oh, no, they must be taught," returned Elsje, looking surprised.

She glanced down at Susie, who was pawing impatiently at Sal and whining for some of her second brownie.

"Willem is now five years old," she added apologetically. "Susie will soon learn."

Sal pushed Susie away, and shook her head doubtfully.

"I don't think she'll ever behave like Willem, however old she gets. She's smart enough. She follows me everywhere, and she meets me at the door after school, but she comes when called only if she's sure it's for something she likes. I'm supposed to give her vitamin drops and brush her every day. She hates both those things. So she just comes to where I can see her but can't reach her. We have to chase her."

Elsje looked shocked.

"That is very bad," she said tartly. "You must not do that—chase her. *Make* her come to you."

Sal squirmed. Elsje had put the lid back on the cooky tin and both dogs had given up hope and galloped away.

"It's not that easy," Sal complained. "I'll show you what it's like trying to '*make* her come.' Come, Susie, come on. Here, Susie."

Susie turned, tail up, tongue out, eyes wary beneath their

thatch. Suddenly good-natured, she trotted in their direction, only to halt just out of Sally's reach and sit down, her tail whacking the ground behind her in a friendly fashion.

"No, you idiot. Come on. Come HERE!" Sal commanded, patting the earth at her side.

Susie cocked her head, looked puzzled, rose as if to obey, gave one final swish of her tail and scampered off, leaving Sal sputtering helplessly.

Elsje had to smile but her words were serious.

"Yes, she needs to be taught. Dogs like to know what they must do," she said.

"Well, I can't teach her, that's for sure." Sal leaned back and let go of her indignation in sudden contentment. "I tell her what to do and she just doesn't. How did you ever teach Willem?"

Elsje did not say anything for a moment. She was watching the two dogs, so different and yet so alike, as they played tag together. When she turned to answer Sally, Sal was taken aback at the change in her expression. Her mouth was a sober line. Her cheeks seemed to redden even as Sal looked at her. She began to tug at her right braid, a gesture which Sal had seen her make in school when an arithmetic problem stumped her or she was having trouble remembering an English word. She kept her eyes on the ground as she spoke, and her voice was strange and halting, as though she were choosing each word with care.

"I did not teach Willem," Elsje said. "Willem is not my dog. My brother Piet—He is the dog of my brother, Pieter. All that Willem knows Piet taught to him while we were still in Holland in our old home. Now I walk Willem. He needs to have walks and I like to take him. But he is still Piet's dog."

12

Something Must Be Wrong with Piet

"PIET'S DOG!" Sal exclaimed.

"Yes," Elsje said, jumping to her feet, as though she wanted to get away from Sally and this new name in the talk between them. "Look, I will show you what Willem has learned."

She stood just in front of Sal and ordered sharply, "Willem, *kom hier.*"

The little dog ran to her at once and sat down before her, his head lifted as though he were waiting for further instructions.

Elsje smiled and bent to stroke him lightly.

"Brave hond. Good dog," she murmured, using both her languages. Then her voice rang out in a new command. "Willem, *blijf daar.*"

Sal looked to see what Willem would do, but this time, it was Elsje who acted. She swung on her heel and walked away from the dachshund. She strode with such energy that Sal could see her pigtails thumping up and down on her shoulder-blades. Willem stayed absolutely still as though he had been glued to the spot where she had left him. "I told him 'Stay there,' " Elsje explained in a swift aside to her audience. Sal clapped for Willem. The little dog did not even turn his head.

Elsje stood for a moment at the end of the Place; then,

once again, ordered Willem to come to her. This time, when she came back, toward Sal, the dog walked along at her left heel as though he were held there by an invisible leash. Elsje walked fast. Willem scurried along, keeping pace. She slowed down till she was barely moving. Willem crawled beside her,

never getting one step ahead of her. At last, they halted in front of Sal.

"Willem, *ga zitten.*"

Willem sat neatly on his haunches.

"Willem, *ga liggen.*"

Willem flattened out, his paws pointing straight in front of him, his dainty face raised to hers.

"Willem, *blijf daar,*" Elsje finished. She dropped down beside Sally while Willem lay patiently, waiting to be dismissed.

"How long will he stay there?" Sal breathed, her eyes wide with respect.

"Till I tell him he can go."

Elsje began praising the little dog, rubbing him gently behind the ears and telling him he was wonderful. Then she let him go and, with a wag of his tail, he was off after Susie.

Sally was overwhelmed. In her mind, she suddenly saw a new Susie, who did all of these things! Susie walking sedately behind her, Susie sitting when told, Susie coming promptly when called . . . Why, if Susie were trained to behave like Willem, she, Sally, would be able to take her out on the leash without having to worry about being yanked off her feet.

Kent and Mindy took turns walking Susie now. The day after Dad had arranged for Sal to feed Susie herself, Melinda, as full of sweetness and good reasons as ever, had offered to walk the dog every day. The two girls had quarreled. When Mindy had said "You can't!" Sal's blood had boiled and she had suddenly hauled off and slapped her older sister. But this time, even Dad had said that Mindy was right. Sal could not control Susie and keep herself from falling at the same time. Now, a scheme was beginning to grow inside Sal's head, as she looked at Elsje.

"That Willem is the smartest dog I have ever seen," she said, at last. "What did you say your brother's name was?"

"Pieter. . . . We call him Piet."

"How did he ever teach Willem all that? How did he begin?"

Elsje relaxed a little. She cupped her hands around her knees and stared off into space.

"It began when Willem was not yet one year," she said dreamily, as though she were telling a beloved story. "I was only just started in school. Piet was always teaching the animals things. He could make the cat we had sit on a chair when she ate. And when he would whistle, she came. It is hard to teach cats."

Sal thought of Purrpuss and nodded. She hadn't learned anything in seven years. She wouldn't even come when you called her unless you had a dish of salmon in your hand maybe.

"He read a book when Willem was a pup. It had pictures of what to do. Willem was very quick to learn, though."

"What did Piet do?"

"He says the same thing over and over—like '*Willem, ga zitten,*' and he makes Willem do it. Then he tells him what a clever dog he is. And when he does it wrong, he tells him how stupid he is and starts all over again."

Sal leaned forward, her wish plain on her face.

"Elsje, would Piet train Susie for me? Do you think he would? It would be so wonderful to be able to say 'Susie, come,' and—"

"No!" Elsje broke in abruptly. "Piet cannot. No! It cannot be."

"But, Elsje—" Sal began, bewildered.

"It cannot be," Elsje repeated stubbornly, refusing to listen.

Her eyes met Sal's. Sal jumped as though she had been stung. Here again was the cold, hard gaze she had faced for the last two weeks in school. Elsje looked away and Sally took a deep breath. Getting Susie trained wasn't worth losing this first friendship.

"Hand me my crutches and let's go in," she said briskly. "You haven't seen my room yet."

"Okay," Elsje cried, scrambling up. Her voice sounded so grateful and happy that Sal decided never to mention Piet again.

Yet, as they crossed the yard, with Willem walking at Elsje's heel and Susie bounding backwards and forwards all over the place, she thought once again what it would be like to have her dog trained to come at her call, to trot beside her. Not looking at Elsje, not saying a word, she wondered what was wrong with Piet.

When they reached the house, Meg came running, her hair flyaway, her shoelaces undone, her overalls, hands and arms black with dirt.

"I've been gardening but I'm all ready to play now," she said hopefully.

Sal could not help laughing.

"Okay," she gave in, "but you'll have to be washed first."

"Oh, it must be wonderful to have a little sister!" Elsje said unexpectedly, as the two of them scrubbed Meg.

Meg herself looked surprised. Nobody had ever said anything like that in her hearing before.

"Brothers are nice too, though," Sal replied, carefully, not looking at her new friend.

"Of course," Elsje said quickly, and became very busy drying Meg's hands with a big towel.

In bed, that night, Sal lay awake, thinking of Piet. Kent had said that nobody liked Piet, and that he would not speak English. Mr. Mackenzie had told her something about Piet too, but then she had been so worried about herself and Elsje that, however hard she tried to remember, she wasn't sure now what he had said. Was it that Piet was sick? Kent had talked as though he were in school—but maybe that was last year. Perhaps now he was home in bed and they were afraid he might die or never walk again or something—and that was why Elsje didn't want to talk about him. He must have been well once, or he couldn't have trained Willem in the first place. Didn't he like dogs any more? Why did Elsje always walk Willem now? Why wouldn't Kent talk to her about Piet that time she had asked?

Sal shivered. Then a new thought hit her.

"Maybe that's it!" she said out loud in the darkness. "Maybe he's gotten crippled somehow—like me!"

The more she thought about it, the more certain she became. That explained why Piet did not take Willem for walks. He probably couldn't manage it on crutches. Perhaps he even had to use a wheelchair. It explained why Elsje hadn't wanted to talk about him, especially to Sal. It even helped to explain why Elsje hadn't wanted to be friends in the beginning. And it finally made sense out of that time she had tried to make Kent tell her about Piet and he had refused and run away from her. He must have thought he would hurt my feelings, telling me about a boy nobody liked who was crippled. . . .

Then Sal forgot about Kent and Elsje and thought about

Piet himself. She had wondered about him before because she had heard that nobody liked him and she had believed nobody liked her. Somehow, she had felt that made a bond between them. But Piet had never been a real live boy in her thoughts, until now. In just one day, she had learned so much more about him. With her own eyes, she had seen his dog and the things he had trained his dog to do. Elsje had made her see the fun he had had teaching even the cat tricks. Now she herself had figured out what had happened, although she still didn't know whether Piet had been in an accident or had been sick or what. Did Mr. Mackenzie say he had been very sick? Anyway, now he was crippled. She pictured him, a thin, light-haired boy with a lonely face, having to sit in a chair at home and watch Elsje start out the door with his dog day after day . . .

When she slept, Sal's face was wet with tears.

At half past eight on Monday morning, Elsje called for her. Under the loving eyes of her family, Sal clumped to the front door without a word. There, she turned, her cheeks very pink, her eyes very bright, and said in a voice that did not sound like her own:

"Good-by! I'll see you at noon."

She felt as though she were bewitched as she set out at Elsje's side. She heard Elsje explain about Libby's cold. Libby was sure she was well enough to come back to school but her mother said that she would have to wait one more day. Sal said that that was too bad. But she still didn't really believe that Elsje was walking to school beside her. At any moment, she knew somebody would break the spell and it would all be over.

"Here we are, Sal," Elsje said, her voice shaking just a little.

Sal knew how she felt. Her own legs were like jelly underneath her, steel braces or no steel braces. What would the kids think when she and Elsje came in together? She had been looking forward to this moment all weekend, but now her stomach was full of somersaulting butterflies. Neither of the girls spoke as they went up the walk.

Nobody from their class was in the hall, surprisingly. Nobody noticed them as they got their coats off and put them away in the lockers. Then, as they turned to go into the classroom, Randy Chisholm came out, bound on an errand for Mr. Mackenzie. When he caught sight of the two coming toward him, side by side, he stopped in his tracks. His lips pursed in a whistle. Sal stiffened angrily but Elsje suddenly giggled.

"We are now friends. Wanna make something out of it?" she growled, doubling up her fists and advancing on Randy.

"No, no! Spare me!" Randy howled, jumping back and throwing up his hands in mock surrender.

Sal laughed and Randy looked at her again. This time, he was grinning.

"Where are you hiding Libby?" he asked. "You can't tell me she isn't in on this."

"'She's home with a cold," Sal said, feeling foolish.

"I knew it!" Randy declared. "Well, it's about time."

Without another word, he was off down the hall. Sal's mouth dropped open.

"What—what did he mean?" she asked Elsje.

"I think Randy means that we should have been friends before," Elsje said, her cheeks reddening. Then, her face brightened. "If Randy thinks we are okay, they will *all* think we are okay," she told Sal. "Let's go in."

Sal found that the worst was already over. Nobody else's stare was as hard to meet as Randy's had been. After she sat down, her legs still sticking out with both knees locked so that she was ready to get herself up for "God Save the Queen," she lifted her head with a new feeling of belonging and caught Mr. Mackenzie's eye. He winked at her.

When the recess bell rang, Elsje stayed behind for a few minutes to talk to the teacher about some work she had handed in. Sal waited for her in the hall. She stood proudly, knowing that Elsje expected her to be waiting there, and she hardly noticed the two boys coming down the corridor. When they drew close to her, however, one of their voices struck such a high, unhappy note that she began listening without meaning to.

"I'm going to tell!" he was insisting. He was a small boy, his round face streaked with tears. "He can't shove me around! Who does he think he is, anyway?"

The bigger boy got in front of him and took hold of his shoulders. He even shook him a little.

"Listen, Luke, LISTEN!" he hissed. "Who started it? Just stop and think of that. If you hadn't gone and opened your big—"

Luke looked daggers at his friend.

"I only said, 'What's the matter, Piet Jansen? Afraid of a little old football?' What's wrong with that? He *is*, isn't he? We need big kids on our team, but he just stands there and sulks. He's scared, and I told him so! He doesn't need to go shoving people into the dirt for telling the truth, does he?"

He broke loose from the grip of the larger boy and ran on down the hall. As their voices died away, one was still trying to persuade the other to forget it—but Sal was no longer listening.

Piet Jansen! Could there be two of them? Hardly. It must be Elsje's brother. But he was at home in a wheelchair. No, he couldn't be. He must be in school. He couldn't even be walking on crutches. Not if Luke thought he ought to be playing football! Unless there was another boy named Piet Jansen. But this school wasn't that big. He must be all right. Yet he couldn't walk his dog. He couldn't train Susie. Elsje had known that without even asking him. Kent wouldn't talk about him. And now, she thought, suddenly taking in what she had just heard, he wouldn't play football with the other kids—and he picked on small boys. She shook her head trying to make the puzzle solve itself. Maybe he's just a really mean boy, she thought. But no. He had taught animals all those things. And Elsje had sounded as though she really loved him, even though something about him worried her.

The boy who had been with Luke came running back down the hall alone. With no idea of what she would say, Sally stepped forward and called.

"Hey!"

"Yeah?" He stared at her, obviously surprised at being spoken to and embarrassed by her crutches.

"Is Piet Jansen Elsje Jansen's brother?" Sal asked hurriedly, aware that Elsje might come out at any moment.

"What's it to you?" the boy asked, edging past her, his eyes suspicious.

"I just want to know. I'm new, that's all, and I just wondered if there were another Piet Jansen." Sal knew her explanation sounded weak but she could not think of anything more convincing.

The boy managed to get by her and took a couple of steps on down the hall before he called back, "He's the only one I ever heard of. Sure, he's her brother, poor girl."

He darted off and left Sal with a mystery which seemed to her to get more mysterious the more she learned about it. She was thinking so hard she forgot why she was standing there. When Elsje said "Hi, let's go!" right beside her, she jumped and looked guilty. Elsje studied her flushed face.

"What is wrong?" she asked.

"Wrong?" Sal echoed, her voice thin. "Nothing's wrong. I—I just saw a couple of little kids who'd been in a fight. Do you know a boy named Luke?"

"Luke McGinnis," Elsje said promptly. "He's always getting into trouble. Then he cries. Do not worry about him, Sally."

It was lucky for Sal that Elsje thought she was upset about Luke. It would have been hard to explain what she really had been wondering about. Piet did not have a motor handicap such as she had. He was not sick in bed. Yet *something* must be wrong with Pieter Jansen. What could it be?

13
Pieter's Side

AFTER SCHOOL, that afternoon, the girls walked as far as Sal's house together. Now November had come the leaves had blown to the ground and the trees along their way lifted clean, dark branches against a pearly sky. The wind was cold. Sal snuggled her chin down into her coat collar and shivered.

"You should come in and get warm," she told Elsje. "I don't have to go for therapy for half an hour."

Elsje shook her head. They were at the end of the Copelands' walk, but she stood poised, ready to be on her way.

"No. I must take Willem for a walk," she said. "And I did not tell my mother I would be late. She worries when we do not come home if we do not tell her first."

Sal ached to ask, "Why do you have to walk Willem? Why doesn't Pieter do it?" But she held her tongue. Elsje headed on up the hill. Sal stood for a moment, watching her go, waving in case she looked back.

I'll never find out about him, she fumed as she went into the house. I don't see how I'll ever know what's wrong!

But that night at supper, when she wasn't even trying to unravel the mystery, when she had not even asked a single question, she heard most of Piet's story.

The rest of the family were already at their places at the table when Kent came storming in. They could hear him

splashing water over his hands (drying the dirt off on a towel, as usual), and then he came charging into the dining room, his eyes blazing.

"Take it easy, boy," Dad warned, as he banged into his chair. "It can't be all that bad."

"That's what *you* think," Kent roared. "I wasn't doing *anything*. You told me not to talk about him, but Jinx and me were just tossing a ball around and it rolled into Jansens' yard—and that great, big . . ."

His next words were lost in furious sobbing. Dad reached

out a big hand and pulled him over against him. Sal felt her throat squeezing tight with sympathy for him, but Melinda gave him a look of pure disgust.

"Honestly, you're the biggest baby," she jeered. "Always bawling about something!"

Kent found his voice again at that. He whirled to face her, still within the circle of Dad's arm.

"I am not!" he yelled. "How would you like it if Pieter Jansen knocked you down when all you did was try to get your ball back? He held it and said it was his because it came in his yard, and I tried to make him give it to me—and . . . And he wouldn't. He's just a great, big bully, that's all! I grabbed it and he shoved me down on the ground and hit me and Jinx kicked him so he had to let me up and we ran. But I hate him. I hate him! I don't care what you say, Dad. He's a big fat slob and he can't even speak English and he didn't even come to school last year—so he's just in Sixth Grade though he's lots bigger than some kids in Junior High! He's stupid and he's—"

"Be quiet, Kent," Dad said. "Pieter Jansen . . ." he went on slowly. "If I have the right family in mind, I believe I know more about Pieter than you do. Do any of you know whether or not Pieter's father's name is Dirk?"

Nobody knew.

"They live in that red brick house on Marlowe Street at the top of the hill," Melinda volunteered.

Dad nodded. "That's Dirk's home," he said. "And Pieter is Elsje's brother, Sally?"

"Yes," Sal said. That was the one thing she had learned for sure about him.

Dad sat back and looked at his family for a long moment.

To the Copelands, that look was as good as a warning. Dad was about to make them "see the other side of the story." Kent, who had subsided into his chair, hardened his heart. There could be no excuse for Piet, no excuse at all. Sal, however, was so excited she could hardly sit still as she waited for Dad to begin.

"It is no wonder that Piet has trouble speaking English," Dad said quietly. "He has been ill almost ever since they arrived here from Holland."

Kent flung his head up suddenly.

"I don't care," he burst out. "He doesn't have to pick on kids half his size!"

"Baby!" Mindy taunted.

"You shut up!" Kent bellowed, lunging toward her. "You—"

Sal glanced at Dad and gave Kent a warning nudge under the table. He turned on her, crimson with fury, but her face was blank. Only the flick of her eyes toward Dad checked him. Shaking with rage, he sat down again. Dad cleared his throat.

"Melinda was right, Kent," he said then. "Your behavior was babyish. Now hold on a minute. Her behavior was no more adult than yours. When a person is grown up, really grown up inside, she would certainly not be either cruel or rude to another person, particularly someone younger than herself. Neither you nor Mindy thought of the other person's point of view. That is one of the chief differences between a child and an adult."

Now Mindy's head drooped over her plate and Sal saw the shine of tears caught in her lashes.

"But this all started with Pieter Jansen," Dad went on. "Try to forget about yourselves for just a few minutes and think about the Jansen family. They had been in Canada only a few days when Piet got a sore throat. They knew no doctor and they knew no English, so his mother put him to bed, thinking it was just a cold, and they waited for it to get better. A week or so later, Piet was aching all over. Mr. Jansen, who had found a job with my company, asked one of the men for the name of a doctor. When Pieter was examined, he was taken to the hospital with rheumatic fever."

"Rheumatic fever!" Mother exclaimed. "Oh, his poor mother!"

"Yes, it was an anxious time for the whole family. They had just arrived, remember. They had very little money and no hospital insurance. So, after a few days in the hospital, Piet was taken home and the doctor, through an interpreter, explained to the Jansens what medicine to give him and how much rest he needed. Piet spent November, December, January, February, March and April mostly in bed."

"Gee!" Kent breathed.

"When he was well enough to go to school, the school year was almost over. He knew hardly any English and he still was supposed to take things easy. The doctor decided that Piet would be better off to wait till September and start off fresh. Pieter still has what they call a 'heart murmur.' He has to get lots of sleep and must stop playing before he gets tired. I don't know what happened when Piet did start school. I do know that, right now, his father is very worried about him."

"But nobody knew—" Kent objected.

"That's not good enough, son. That's my excuse too, and it is a poor one. Dirk Jansen is a brave man. He had a construction company much like mine in Holland, but nobody is building new houses there. More and more young people are leaving Holland and going to live in other countries where there will be room for them to build homes of their own and where they feel there will be more choice of a future. Dirk thought ahead and decided he wanted Elsje and Piet to be able to grow up and get married and bring up children without having to move too far away from him and his wife. So, without knowing English and without much money, he came to this country for the sake of his children's future.

"Right away, his son became seriously ill. His money was eaten up by medical bills. The only job he could get was a much poorer one than the one he had in Holland. And I didn't even know that anything was wrong! After Piet had been ill for two months, Dr. Brewster mentioned his case to me. It was only then that I questioned Dirk and so opened the door for him to tell me of the trouble he was having.

"And yet, Dirk Jansen likes Canada. He wants to learn English, in spite of the fact that he finds it very difficult. The men laughed at him, at first, but now they are all helping him correct his mistakes. He wants to get his debts paid off. He is eager to make friends, and he makes them wherever he goes. He is going to night school and he plans on becoming a Canadian citizen."

Dad paused, looking around at the circle of faces turned to him.

Then he turned to Kent and said gently: "Dirk is acting in a grown-up way, son, and Pieter, for reasons I think you can guess, is acting like a child. And it doesn't have to be that way just because Piet is a boy and his dad is a man. Lots of men act like children. And often, children act grown-up. Meg is grown-up when you torment her and she stands up for her own rights instead of running and tattling. Melinda was grown-up the day we moved and she was invited to spend the day at the lake, but she chose to stay home and help. Sally was grown-up when she said she'd take Susie to be hers, because she saw Susie was afraid and needed loving, even though, right then, she herself was terrified of dogs. And Kent, when you painted the garage roof, and it took you twice as long as you figured and meant missing that hike, and you stuck with it till the job was done—you were grown-up that day."

"But why did Piet have to shove me?" Kent got out, his voice thick with tears.

"I don't know why, Kent," Dad answered, honestly. "But stopping to find out why is the first and most important thing you can do. My heavens! I have to get out of here. I'm due at a board meeting. I talk too much."

"I'll get your coat," Mother said, and they left the room in a hurry.

For a moment, the children stayed in their places, not looking at each other.

Then Kent jumped up. "I wish you'd mind your own business!" he whispered at Melinda.

He was already at the door when Mindy's voice reached him.

"I'm sorry," she said.

Sal knew how they both were feeling. Whenever Dad talked to you like that, it made living seem so much harder, and yet more exciting too. He made you want to turn yourself into a different kind of person—but you didn't want anybody to see you feeling that way.

Susie put her paw on Sal's lap, asking for a bite of something. She did that only when Dad had left the room. He had a strict rule that dogs shouldn't be fed at the table. Sal scratched the soft, upstanding ears.

"There's nothing left, Suse," she said sympathetically. "Only some of Kent's chocolate pudding, and you wouldn't like that."

Meg had scrambled down and gone high-tailing it after Dad and Mother. Now Melinda looked wonderingly at Sal.

"Were you really scared of dogs?" she asked.

Sal flushed.

"I guess so," she admitted, at last, "but Susie was . . ."

"Yeah, I know," Mindy said with a little grin. "Susie was different."

She rose, leaned over to give Susie a pat and went away to her room. Sal, reaching for her crutches, thought: Boy, we sure are quiet when Dad gets through with us!

Then she began to think about Piet again—only now most of the mystery was gone. Of course Dad had scolded Kent for talking about Piet the way he had that first time, before she started school; that was why Kent wouldn't talk about him to her when she had asked. And Piet had a 'heart murmur.' That was what was wrong with him.

Only that didn't explain why he didn't like Willem any more! And why did he pick on little kids like Luke and Kent? Was he a bully or had all that had happened to him made him unhappy? Like Susie, was he "different," needing someone to be nice to him?

She stopped short.

I'm doing it! she thought. I'm asking "Why?" the way Dad told us to. . . . Then she laughed. . . . *But I still can't figure out the answers!*

14

Please, Susie!

LIBBY CAME BACK, as gay and friendly and Libbyish as ever. When the three girls walked to the playground together, at recess time, chattering and laughing, Sally felt sure she would never be unhappy again.

Then she heard a voice shout: "We need Libby. Hurry up!"

All at once, Sal was afraid. Sunshine was pouring down on the schoolyard, as though summer had decided to come back for just one more day, and the other children were already playing a rousing game of Red Rover to celebrate. One side was getting badly beaten and these were the boys and girls who were calling to Libby, and now to Elsje too, to come and join them.

"You go on," Sal said, surprising herself more than anyone else. "I'll watch."

"No, we cannot!" Elsje called to the waiting team, even while Sal was speaking. "We are busy."

Then she beckoned Libby and Sal over to the edge of the playground.

"My mother says to ask if you will come to my house to eat supper with us tomorrow evening," she said. "I have told her about you and she wants to meet you."

Sal thought, at first, that she was the one Mrs. Jansen wanted to meet, for she must have had Libby over often in the months she and Elsje had been friends. But Libby too was looking surprised as well as pleased.

"My mother does not know very much English," Elsje added. She raised her head proudly. "She has been in the house too much and she has been busy. But she does want to meet you," she repeated.

Sal understood, suddenly, that Elsje was worried about having them as guests. She remembered how she had felt standing outside the Place, uncertain whether or not Elsje would like it.

"It will be nice to see Willem again," she said warmly.

Elsje's face brightened.

"You can bring Susie to the supper too!" she exclaimed. "My mother likes little dogs very much."

Sal looked doubtful. She didn't know what her mother would have to say to that. But, with or without Susie, she was happy at the invitation. She swung both her feet off the ground at once, which was her way of giving a skip of delight.

"We'll ask our mothers, but I'm positive mine will say it's fine," Libby promised.

That afternoon, Sally had her great idea. What put it into her head she did not know. Perhaps it was Elsje's invitation, for she had just finished telling Mother about it and Mother had said "How wonderful!" So Piet was in her mind—Piet and Willem, because she was still bursting with questions about them. She was sitting on the edge of her bed, still in her school clothes—a crisp snowy blouse and a green plaid skirt—and she was wondering what Pieter looked like. Kind of tall, she guessed, and thin, with dark, sad eyes and a white face.

Then Susie sprang up on the bed and started a game of let's-see-who-can-push-the-other-one-over-first.

"Get off me!" Sal yelped, shoving at the ball of lively fur

with both hands. "Quit it, you nuisance! Okay, okay, I'll scratch you."

She rolled Susie over and began scratching her stomach, while Susie smiled up at her meltingly and waggled her paws.

Sal smiled back. "You're a goof, did you know it?" she murmured lovingly. "Why aren't you like Willem? Then I'd just say 'Down,' only in Dutch, and you'd stop bothering me."

That was when the idea struck. "I know what I'll do," she said, her voice going up. "I'll train you myself! I'll do it secretly, and surprise everybody!" She reached for Susie in a way that meant business. "And we'll begin right now!" she finished.

Susie squirmed but stayed, hopefully, tummy-side-up. Sal let go of her for a moment and considered.

"Sit!" she decided. "I'll teach you to sit first."

Susie wagged her tail as best she could, being still upside down. Sal looked uneasy, but the light of battle still gleamed in her blue eyes.

"Okay, I'll start with 'Roll over' instead," she muttered. "Roll over, Susie."

Susie still wagged and waited to be scratched. Sal sighed. There was nothing for it but to turn her over by force. She clutched the furry body in both hands and began to hoist and push. Susie was puzzled and far from pleased. She turned over of her own free will, but so quickly that she got loose from Sal's grasp. Making sure Sal was watching, she stalked off a couple of paces and curled up on one side, her back to her mistress, her tail tucked disapprovingly between her feet.

Sal waited for a minute. Then she put both hands under the little dog from behind and heaved. Susie rose, in spite of herself, gave one injured look over her shoulder, and leaped, landing upright at last, but out of reach, on the floor.

"Oh, drat!" Sally exclaimed. She slid her feet to the rug beside the small dog. The small dog at once backed away. Whatever this was all about, she was growing more and more sure that she wanted nothing to do with it.

"Come on, Susie," Sal was forced to coax. "I'm not going to hurt you, honest. Come on, Susie. Please!"

She knew, and Susie knew, that unless Susie would let herself be caught the training was all over. Susie had long since mastered the art of staying out of reach. She paid no attention to the small brown hand held out to her nor to the soft, peace-making voice. Her tail wagging not at all now, she edged away still further, distrust written all over her.

Sal flopped back on the bed as though Susie did not interest her any longer. Sometimes, she knew, trickery worked when flattery failed. If she pretended well enough, Susie might decide the coast was clear and come back. Across the room, Susie sat down with a small thud. Sal, staring at the ceiling, heard her and knew, without daring to look, that Susie was waiting to see what was up. Sal sighed loudly and went on looking at the ceiling.

A minute passed. Another. It seemed as though she'd been lying there for at least half an hour. Her leg twitched and in about two seconds she was going to have to scratch it and forget the whole thing. Then, she heard Susie's nails begin to click slowly across the floor. A wet nose snuffled at her ankle. A sliver of tongue gave her a careful lick.

Sal rolled over and swung her legs up onto the bed with the rest of her. She put her head over the edge and eyed the small terrier. The eyes peering up at her were baffled and mournful. Also there lurked in them some of her own exasperation.

"Poor Susie," Sal crooned, giving up all thought of training her for a second. "Do you want your tummy scratched?"

Instantly, the dog was into the box and up onto the bed. A moment later, they were exactly as they had been before Sally had had her idea, Sal busily scratching, Susie lazily waving her paws in the air and looking pleased.

But Sarah Jane Copeland was not one to give up that easily. Four times more, she tried, somehow getting Susie up on all fours, once even getting her into a sitting position, before the little dog collapsed like a piece of wet spaghetti. Sal was hampered by the need to keep a firm hand on Susie's collar to prevent escape. Between Susie's unwillingness and Sal's having to work with one hand, the training was an ordeal for both of them. After an hour, Susie, desperate at last, lunged extra hard and got away. Then mistress and dog glared at each other from opposite sides of the room.

Susie's coat was standing up every which way. She was shaking, but more with anger than in fear. Every time Sal stirred, she shifted, trying to retreat further into the wall. Her collar had been pulled up high about her ears when she jumped and a more miserable, misused-looking dog it would have been hard to find.

Sal was also the worse for wear. She had forgotten all about changing out of her good blouse and skirt. Now the blouse was rumpled and grimy while the skirt was as askew as Susie's collar. She had pleaded with Susie, tricked her, chased her and cornered her once, held on to her for dear life, ordered, coaxed, threatened and shouted—and here they were. The room was between them and Sal knew that she couldn't catch the dog again whatever she tried. They were both out of breath and upset. Her clothes were a mess and Mother would be cross—and worst of all, Susie had not learned a thing and Sal's wonderful idea was no good at all!

"Oh, darn you anyway!" she cried at the dog across from her. "Why can't you do anything right? You're just stupid!"

Susie just looked at her. That look was more than Sal could bear. With a groan of defeat, she let herself fall back on the bed again, too tired even to cry.

Dusk filled the bedroom. Meg came running in and stopped as she caught sight of Sally lying stretched out in grim silence.

"Are you crying, Sal?" she asked, at last, her small voice uncertain.

Sal lay still for one more second and then reared up, her face twisting. "No, I'm *not* crying! Why should I be crying, for heaven's sake? I'm not sad. I wouldn't cry for anybody—"

Tears spilled down her cheeks in a sudden storm, making a liar out of her. Meg scurried away through the darkness, calling for Mother. Mother arrived and the world began to come straight again. She flipped the light switch briskly, took one look at Sal's red, tear-washed face and sent Meg, who was hovering in her wake, for a "wet but not dripping" washcloth. Then, without another word, she reached down her cool hands and cupped them around Sal's blazing cheeks. Sal lay still. She could not trust her voice to speak. But Mother's smile and touch began to drive the misery from her eyes. At last, she managed a feeble grin of her own.

"That's better," Mother said. "Give me your hand now."

She swung Sal to a sitting position. Meg came back with the washcloth and Mother wiped away all traces of tears. Then, without asking any questions about what on earth had happened to them, she helped Sal out of her skirt and blouse and into her pajamas and dressing gown.

"Now, let's see if we can get a little action around here," she said. "Get your hair brushed, Sal, and then attend to Susie's supper. It's time we were having ours."

Sal looked at Susie. With her instinct for knowing when danger was past, Susie came trotting across the room.

"She's all ruffled up!" Meg exclaimed, squatting down beside her and patting her coat down.

Sal pretended she did not hear.

The rest of the family had almost finished the first course by the time she got to the table.

"Excuse me for being late," she said to Dad as she took her place.

Dad gazed at her pajamas and dressing gown.

"You're excused," he replied, "but you look early to me."

They were having Sal's favorite supper, macaroni and cheese. Mother passed her plate and there was lots of the crusty top part Mother must have saved for her. Sal looked around. Melinda and Kent were arguing about what they would do if they woke up one morning and were told that the school had burned down. Meg was listening dreamily, a ring of milk around her mouth. Dad took a stalk of celery —and Mother passed him the salt without being asked. Susie finished her dinner, came in, looked apologetically at Dad, and lay down sneakily by Sal's chair.

All at once, Sal was so happy she had to do something. She wanted to sing out at the top of her lungs, "I think this is the most wonderful family in the entire world!" But, instead, she leaned sideways and whispered very softly, "I'm sorry I said you were stupid."

Susie's tail swept back and forth joyfully, and peace was made.

15

Piet Himself

"WE'LL LOOK like Christmas come early," Sal said, glancing from her own scarlet pleated skirt, spread out on the bed beside her, to Libby in her Kelly-green corduroy jumper.

Libby nodded, but Sal could see she had something else on her mind. Dad had agreed to drive the two of them to the Jansens' and Libby was waiting for Sal to finish dressing. She sat sideways in the captain's chair, her back propped against one arm, her spindly legs draped over the other. Sal did up the buttons on her blouse. There were only two of them and they were easy ones. They were made of mother-of-pearl and they caught bits of blue and green and rose in them when you looked at them in different lights. One of Libby's feet clonked impatiently against the chair and Sal stopped admiring her buttons and reached hurriedly for her skirt.

"I'm almost ready," she said, hauling it over her head and adjusting the straps on her shoulders.

This time, Libby didn't even nod.

"Sal," she said suddenly, "have you ever seen Piet?"

"No." Sal's eyes were full of questions.

Libby wriggled in the chair as though she had grown uncomfortable all at once.

"He's kind of . . ." she started. Then she stopped and began again. "Except for Elsje, I don't know the Jansens really. Mr. Jansen is away at work and Elsje's mother is . . . shy, I guess

. . . I've just seen Piet when I've gone to pick up Elsje . . . He . . . I don't really know him, but . . ."

Sal was dressed, but she sat still, waiting for Libby to finish. When no other words came, she prodded.

"But what?"

"Oh, I don't know," Libby evaded. She saw with obvious relief that Sal was ready, and stood up. "Come on," she urged, "let's get going."

Sal gathered up her crutches and followed. So Pieter had Libby puzzled too! Even though she had met him and spoken to him! What was it about him that was so different?

Elsje's family rented the downstairs of a tall red brick house. There were no steep steps to struggle up, but the big, dark door looked forbidding and unfriendly. As Dad got her crutches out of the car, Sal was suddenly thankful he was there. Libby strolled up the walk as though she were sure she would feel at home anywhere in the world. Susie, tugging on a leash Libby held, did not seem anxious at all.

It was a miracle that Susie had, at last, been allowed to come. When the idea had first been suggested, Mother had said "No!"

"Over my dead body will you take that pup along!" she had continued, glowering at them as though she could not imagine what nonsense they would think of next. "Why, that poor woman will have her hands full with you and Libby without having to look after your livestock!"

Libby was the one who had changed her mind. Libby had a gift for talking grownups around. She had stood in the kitchen, slouched sideways, with one hand on her hip, and grinned engagingly at Mother.

"You know, Mrs. Copeland, I think Elsje feels kind of

scared about having us over," she said. "Maybe it's because her mother doesn't know much English. When she had the idea of us bringing Susie, she looked all pleased and she told us her mother just loved little dogs. And the first thing she said in school, this morning, was that her mother said bringing Susie would be fine. So I think it might be easier if—"

"Stop, Libby!" Mother begged. "I might as well give in now, for I know you'll go on till I do. Susie may go. But you two see that she behaves herself! And for goodness' sake, take her for a walk in the back yard last thing before you leave!"

Dad went to the door with them. Then he said he would call for them about eight o'clock, and left with a quick good-by. Sal's insides seemed to have gone away and left her empty and cold, as she waited for the door to open. Until that moment, she had been so eager to see Elsje's family, Piet especially, that she had forgotten they were all strangers. Now she wanted to run away, but Libby had long ago banged the knocker, and at that very moment Elsje was swinging back the door.

The three girls smiled at each other. Elsje was dressed up too, in a soft blue dress with a lace collar which made her look less matter-of-fact than usual. Her braids had been looped up and tied with blue ribbons. She stood a little stiffly, as though being a hostess awed her, but the brightness of her smile showed how glad she was to see them.

"Mother," she called over her shoulder. "They are here. It is Libby and Sal."

Mrs. Jansen came bustling up behind her daughter. Sal could feel her face redden as Elsje's mother looked at her. When you were at home or at school, she thought unhappily, where everybody was used to seeing you, you forgot all about having cerebral palsy. Only once in a blue moon, when something startled you and you jumped harder than anyone else and your pencil flew out of your hand, or when the tip of your crutch slipped in some wet leaves and you fell flat on your face unexpectedly, or when everybody was waiting for you and you couldn't get the knee-lock of your brace done up, did you remember. But when you went to strange places and people looked at you the way Mrs. Jansen was looking, with sorry, extra-kind eyes, then you had to remember and feel different.

"Come in, why don't you?" Elsje said, nudging her mother, as though to make room for the girls to get past.

Mrs. Jansen stopped looking at Sally. Instead, her eyes lit on Susie and she beamed.

"Oh, *wat een Lief hondje,*" she murmured in Dutch, leaning down and holding out her hand for Susie to sniff. Susie wagged her tail just as hard at Dutch as she did at English, Sal noticed. Then Willem arrived, recognized Susie at once, and wiggled happily.

"I'll have to introduce my pooch to your two," Libby said, as Mrs. Jansen hurried off to her kitchen again and Elsje took the girls' coats. "He's about twice as wide as Willem. He doesn't walk any more. He waddles!"

Elsje looked severe.

"You should put him on a diet," she said sternly.

Sal laughed. She was glad that Susie wasn't the only dog Elsje thought needed reforming.

"Heck, I could stop feeding that dog altogether and he'd stay fat as butter," Libby defended herself. "My Grandma gives him cookies and scraps all day long when I'm at school. She thinks I starve him."

Even Elsje laughed at that, although she still looked as though she thought Libby ought to get busy and change her grandmother too if that would thin down the dog. Susie, freed from the leash, followed Willem through the nearest door, and the three girls went along after them.

There, caught in the act of leaving the room at the sound of their coming, stood Piet Jansen.

At first glance, Sal could not believe that this was the boy she had been wanting to see for what seemed such a long time. But Libby said "Hi, Piet," and he bobbed his head in reply.

He was fat. That was the first thing that struck Sally. She had been so sure he would be thin and pale and sad-looking. But, instead, he was stocky, with round, rosy cheeks. His hair didn't hang down over his forehead in a soft wave the way she had expected. It was reddish and was clipped off in a bristling crew-cut. He didn't look happy, but neither did he look sad the way she had pictured him. He looked angry—angry and very unfriendly.

"This is Sal Copeland," Elsje introduced them. "Sal, this is my brother Piet."

"Hello," Sal managed, still staring at him.

"Hello," he said, scowling back.

He would have left the room then, but turning quickly toward the other door, he practically tripped over Susie. He paused. Her ears lowered, her tail stiff as a poker, the little dog sniffed at the cuff of his jeans, while Willem watched tensely, ready to rush to Piet's defense if Susie forgot herself. The boy's face softened. He stood perfectly still, letting Susie make certain he was someone who ought to be allowed to stay. Lapsing into Dutch, just as his mother had done earlier, he murmured, *"Lieve hond . . . brave hond."*

He *is* nice, after all, Sal thought with relief.

"I don't know what you told her," she said to him, "but I bet she understood you. Her name is Susie."

Piet jerked upright as though he had been shot. There was no mistaking the scorn that flashed in his eyes as they fell on her. Without a word, he turned on his heel and left the room. Willem started after him, but Elsje, her voice unsteady, called him back.

"You have a visitor," she reminded him, trying hard to sound as though nothing had gone wrong. "You can't leave Susie, Willem. Sit down, Sal. Libby, sit here."

She herself sat down on the couch. Susie jumped up beside her. Then, she turned and peered anxiously over the edge at Willem, who was too long of body and too short of leg to join her. The girls broke into laughter and Elsje lovingly gathered the dachshund up and gave him a boost onto the couch. With a waywardness Sal well remembered from their training session the day before, Susie instantly deserted both couch and Willem and sprang to the rug again. Willem sighed, but, polite as always, followed, and a wild game of tag was started, Susie dashing around looking for furniture to hide behind while Willem trotted doggedly after her.

The Jansens' living room, with its heavy rented furniture and brown walls, was very different from the one in Sal's home. For a moment or two, she felt uncomfortable there, but then, what with laughing at the dogs and talking about school, she forgot about it. She was surprised when Mrs. Jansen called them to wash their hands for supper.

Since the Jansens shared an upstairs bathroom, Sal and Libby washed at the kitchen sink. Elsje's mother hovered over them. Suddenly, Sal's left crutch slipped a little. Automatically, Sal reached to anchor it more firmly, but as she did so, Mrs. Jansen grabbed her elbow. Sal, clutching at the sink to keep her balance, was dismayed to see how distressed and worried she looked.

"It's okay," she blurted. "I can take care of myself all right."

Elsje rattled off a long, scolding sentence in Dutch and Mrs. Jansen backed away, looking miserable. Sal felt miserable too. First she hadn't wanted anyone to fuss over her. Now, she had hurt someone and made herself stand out more than ever just by trying to be independent. She gulped, vowing fiercely not to cry and make everything ten times worse. Dragging her gaze up from the floor, she found herself face to face with Piet. He had come in just in time to hear her words to his mother and she caught a strange, new expression on his face as their eyes met and held. It was almost as though he understood.

Now he likes me, Sal thought, bewildered.

She followed Libby into the dining room and there was introduced to Elsje's father. He was short with a ruddy, full face. He said little but he looked in friendly fashion from one to the other as Elsje presented Sal and reminded him who Libby was. Mr. Jansen didn't seem to see her crutches at all.

Now that her father was there, Elsje was more at ease. When her mother said something to her in Dutch, she laughed. "It's all right," she said. Then, turning to Sal, she explained.

"She is worried in case the chair will be too high for you. Hurry up and sit down."

After that, of course, one of her knee-locks stuck and Libby had to help her. Then the chair was heavy and Sal couldn't get it moved up to the table. Mr. Jansen came quickly to push her in, just as Dad would have done, but still, the seconds before he came seemed long to Sal. Her hand was shaking as she took the plate of meat Libby passed to her. Bravely she faced up to eating unfamiliar food. All sort of meats and cheeses and various spreads were on the table and everyone was filling his own plate to suit himself. The knives were heavy and Sal tore a hole in her bread as she tried to spread it. The room was stuffy and hot. Her cheeks seemed to be on fire. In spite of Libby's chatter and Mr. Jansen's answers, everything about the meal seemed strained, to Sally, as though it were never going to end. Finally, worst of all, she reached for something and knocked over a little pitcher of sauce, making a dark pool on the snowy tablecloth. Mrs. Jansen clucked with distress, "just like a hen," Sal thought wretchedly, and this time she knew she was going to cry.

It was Piet who saved her. He had not said a word since they sat down, except for a low *"Dank je wel, Moeder,"* when his mother poured him a glass of milk. But now he spoke suddenly and clearly.

"How old is this Susie?"

Sal gave him one look of sheer gratitude. Miraculously, the tears were gone before they arrived. Even Mrs. Jansen, mopping up the sauce, seemed unexpectedly a friend, as she looked at her son, her eyes lighting up in a smile.

Piet's nice—Sal told herself, her interest in him kindling again—he said that on purpose to help me. He MUST be nice!

She answered him eagerly. "She's almost nine months old

now. Just a pup really. I sure wish, though, that she could do all the things that Willem can."

She waited for Piet to say something, but he was silent.

His father said gently, smiling at her, "It takes time to teach dogs to be as smart as Willem is, Sally. Your dog will learn."

"Well," Sal said, remembering her try at teaching Susie, "I want to train her, but—"

Piet interrupted. His voice struck out at her like a blow, scornful and bitter.

"You!" he scoffed. "You! You cannot train her—you are . . . *kreupel.*"

16

The Quarrel

NOBODY had to translate for Sally. She knew Piet had said that she was crippled. She sat very still, looking at him quite steadily. It was as though a spell had been cast over her, for she felt like somebody else entirely, somebody strange and cold and queer.

"Well, you aren't crippled. Why don't you train her for me?" she asked.

There was an instant of utter silence. Then Elsje drew in one small, sharp breath, while Mrs. Jansen broke into a flood of Dutch in which Sal felt as though she were drowning. She did not see Elsje's father raise his hand, but suddenly the silence was back. One of the dogs whimpered anxiously. Piet's hands were clenching the table edge and Sal saw how white his knuckles were, while she waited for him to answer.

"I am. I am crippled too—like you. I cannot train any more dogs; I am just as crippled as you."

"No, Piet," his mother cried, but he went on, his voice almost hysterical.

"I do not want to do it anyway. I cannot do it—and I do not want to anyway."

"But I *do* want to, and I *can!*" Sally said.

She could not believe it was herself speaking. The words had come from her in a new strong way, as though she had some secret power. Her chin was high and her eyes flashing proudly. Had she but known it, both Libby and Elsje were staring at her as though she were a stranger. Nor was she finished.

"I started training Susie yesterday," she said. "I don't really need you to help me at all. I wouldn't want your help."

She had forgotten all about the struggle of the day before, all about the fact that she was certain she would never be able to teach Susie.

"Anyway, you aren't really crippled at all," she finished. "If you want to know the truth, I think you're just scared!"

Mr. Jansen's hand closed over hers and she faltered. Suddenly, she was horribly frightened by what she had said. Pieter sprang to his feet. For a second, Sal did not know whether he was going to hurl something at her or run from the room, but his father's other hand caught his wrist and drew him back down to his chair.

"Now that is enough," he said. "Look at your dogs! You are making them troubled." He gave Sal a grave smile and pointed to Susie. "It is a good thing that you train this Susie. She wants to have my dinner. She will make me, how do you say it? . . . Bones and skin?"

He sucked in his cheeks, trying to look as though he were starving. Susie still waited hopefully. Mr. Jansen shook his head, his face mournful. Then, slipping her a bite from his plate, he warned, "*Sh,* Susie. Do not tell." He looked so sneaky—and yet he had done it openly—Sal laughed in spite of the way her insides were all tied up in knots. Piet, white-faced and silent, picked up his fork and pretended nobody else was in the room.

Elsje suddenly sat back in her chair and gave a sigh of relief as though, at that moment, she had put down a heavy burden. Then, just as suddenly, she smiled across the table at Sally.

"After we finish eating," she said gaily, turning her head so that her smile included her mother, "Libby and Sal and I will do the dishes, *Moeder,* while you play for us on the piano."

"Oh, no," Mrs. Jansen protested. She was obviously searching for more words but could not find them. "No, no, Els," she repeated.

Sal saw then how pretty Elsje's mother was. While Piet and she had been quarreling, Mrs. Jansen had flushed bright red, and it was partly her look of horror that had brought Sally back to herself. But now, under the magic of her husband's nonsense and Elsje's talk about her wonderful way with a piano, she blossomed into a different person. Her eyes sparkled and her cheeks were a lovely pink. Around her face, bits of hair which had been combed back loosened and curled softly in the heat.

So many changes in herself and everyone around her were making Sally tired clear through. She gave up pretending to eat and just sat listening as Mr. Jansen, Libby and Elsje kept the conversation going smoothly. The minute his father rose from the table, Piet got up and slipped from the room, Willem going after him like a small, brown shadow.

Maybe he doesn't like Willem, Sal thought, watching them leave, but Willem sure loves him. Elsje walks that dog every day and brushes him and everything, and yet, if Piet's in the room, Willem never even looks at her.

Then she forgot about Piet, for Libby was handing her her crutches and Elsje was ordering her to get out to the sink and start working. As she clutched her dish towel, she was filled with dread. All along, the evening had been doomed. Now she was surely going to drop and break half of the Jansens' best china. But Libby tactfully managed to leave the knives and forks and spoons for her to dry while she did the glasses and plates. It was Elsje who broke a dish, as she tried to wash fast enough to keep two driers busy.

Mrs. Jansen stayed at the piano until that moment, but the crash of one of her dinner plates brought her scurrying to the kitchen. Sal could tell she wasn't really too upset, because Mr. Jansen and Elsje laughed at her as she scolded them in Dutch, but she whisked her daughter out of the way,

all the same, and washed the rest of the dishes herself.

Before Mrs. Jansen joined them, the girls had been too busy working and listening to the music from the piano to talk.

Now Elsje coaxed, "Sing for us, *Moeder.*"

"I will not," Mrs. Jansen said, shaking her head and washing dishes so hard the suds flew.

"Please," begged Elsje.

Her mother kept on refusing, saying she knew no English songs, but when Elsje insisted that that was one of the very reasons she wanted her mother to sing, so that Libby and Sal could hear some songs in Dutch, she at last gave in. Sitting there polishing away at the heavy spoons with the curlicued handles, Sal was in a new world. Mrs. Jansen's voice was warm and sweet. Sometimes, you could tell the songs were funny, and you laughed. Sometimes, they made you feel dreamy and sad and your hands slowed down till you were hardly working at all. Not knowing what the words meant made them all the more magical.

Once, the spell was broken for a moment. From another room, there came the sound of a chair being shoved back. Mrs. Jansen's song died and the group in the kitchen was silent. Everybody knew that Piet, all by himself, except for Willem, was somewhere having to listen to their music. Sal knew that it was her fault. If she hadn't . . .

Then, Elsje demanded another song, in a strong clear voice, as though nothing had happened. Her father took it up. "Yes, please, Mrs. Jansen," Libby said. The magic began again.

They hardly got the dishes out of the way before Dad was at the door. Sal could not believe that it was almost eight o'clock, although at suppertime she felt as though she had already been there for hours. Getting into her coat, she wondered, wearily, if she would ever be invited to Elsje's house again. Maybe Elsje wouldn't even want to be friends any longer tomorrow. They had not really had a chance to speak together since she and Piet had quarreled. Sal kept her gaze on Susie, on Dad, on her coat, on everything but Elsje's face until they were actually on their way out the door.

Then she had to make sure that things were all right between them. She turned and looked back, directly at Elsje—and found Elsje looking straight at her in return. Sal had no idea what the look in Elsje's eyes meant, but she did know she had never seen that particular look before.

There was nothing much they could say in front of Mr. and Mrs. Jansen, but suddenly Elsje, still staring at Sally in that new way, took a step toward her and said quickly, "I have an idea, Sally. I will tell you tomorrow."

Encouraged, but still bewildered, Sal nodded in reply and the door swung shut behind her.

17

Elsje's Plot

ELSJE was not angry, the next morning, but she was still different. Whenever Sally looked up, in the middle of studying spelling words, figuring out fractions or reading a book, Elsje was looking at her. She always gave a little grin and looked away when Sal caught her. But why was she staring like that in the first place?

Nothing happened at recess. Elsje just looked at Sal some more and seemed a little more eager than usual to arrange that the three of them meet after school. If she had something special to do, she gave them no hint of what it was.

By lunchtime, Sal was thoroughly uneasy. She even tried to tell the family about it, but she couldn't make them understand. They kept asking silly questions, like, "What do you mean—'looks' at you?"

"She just looks at me, that's all."

"Maybe she thinks you stole the silverware last night," Kent guessed through a mouthful of mashed potatoes.

"Maybe you're looking at her all the time and that's what makes her look at you," Mindy said.

That sounded sensible, but Sally knew it wasn't true because she kept catching Elsje's eye, not Elsje catching hers.

"Just be patient, dear," Mother advised. "She's probably got some idea and she's waiting till school's over to tell you."

Mother was right, yet even when school was out, Elsje

waited a long time to begin. It wasn't until the three of them were safely in the Place, bundled up in blankets, the tips of their noses pink in the November wind, that Elsje said:

"Sal, you must train Susie."

Sal stared at her blankly, not believing her ears. Then, seeing how intent and sober her friend's eyes were, she answered just as seriously.

"I don't know what you mean . . . I mean, I don't know why it matters, but I can't train her. I've tried already. She won't do anything I tell her. Is . . . have you been thinking about me training Susie all day? Is that what you were talking about last night?"

Her voice showed her astonishment and Elsje sighed. Then she turned a little, shrugging her shoulders free of blankets, so that she could face both the others.

"I must tell you about Piet," she said. "I do not think I will be able to explain very well, but you must understand.

"I have told you how Pieter is good with dogs. Not just with dogs, with all animals. My uncle in Holland helped him. My uncle is a *dierenarts*—an animal doctor. He gave Willem to Piet. Piet even named Willem after him. Our neighbors once had a big dog that bit at the children on the street and growled. They were going to kill him, but Piet, he said "No." Every day, he spent time with that dog. He made that dog so that he was safe for children to play with. Whenever Piet was home, Willem and the neighbor's dog, Bello, walked right behind him.

"In those days Piet planned when he was a man to go on working with animals. Maybe to be a doctor like my Uncle Willem. Maybe, he said, train animals for a circus. He made friends with some other boys and they worked with their dogs together. Then, my father decided we should come to Canada."

Elsje paused to draw a deep breath. Libby and Sal said nothing. They were too absorbed to interrupt.

"Pieter got sick before it was time to begin school here even. The doctor said it was rheumatic fever and that Piet must stay in bed." She hesitated, "It . . . it was hard for Pieter and for my mother too. It was hard also for my father and for me, but soon my father went to work and I went to school. We were learning English. We were making friends. But Piet had to stay in the house, and when some women came to be friendly to my mother, she was afraid, knowing no English, and she—she acted as though she did not want to know anyone here. When they came back again, she was afraid and she did not answer the door. They did not come again. Then, my mother was always crying and Piet got so he would hardly speak to anybody. He talks Dutch to my mother, but whenever my father or I say something in English, he looks away."

Just telling about it, Elsje's voice grew husky with tears. The others girls stared at the ground, wishing they were somewhere else because neither of them knew what to say or do.

"Piet cannot take Willem for walks, so I must do it. Soon he is talking as though Willem is my dog, not his. Only Willem always will love Piet the best. For a while, he gets letters from the boys in Holland and he gets Mother to write to them for him, but then, I guess they are busy with school and their dogs because the letters stop coming except once in a long time. No Canadian boys come to see him, he has never gone to school. No boys here know him. My mother gets so sad for him and Piet gets sad too. She cooks him all the foods he likes best, the ones we had in Holland. She reads him all our Dutch books over and over. It is almost as though they are both still living in our old home.

"Then, the doctor says that Piet can begin to get up. He says he can walk, but not run too much, not get too tired. His heart is hurt by the rheumatic fever. The doctor says not to be sad, that Piet can be like other boys, just that he will not play football and not run so much. But Piet, he always has liked to run and to play football."

With a jolt, Sal remembered what had happened when Kent's football rolled onto the Jansens' lawn, what had happened when Luke McGinnis had teased Piet about being afraid to play.

"But, though he was better, Piet was not the same any longer," Elsje was going on. She looked from one to the other as though she were willing them to understand what she was saying and believe it. "He used to be . . . Oh, he was quiet, but always busy with new plans, laughing, liking to do things, liking people. . . . But now, he says he is too sick to want to do the things he used to. He only goes to school because the doctor says he has to, but when he comes home, he hides himself in the house. My father tells him he should go out, make friends, but my mother is sorry for him. She is afraid for him, that he will be sick again. She is alone without friends too and so she lets him stay in with her. When I said he should walk Willem now, he said he could not. He said he was not well enough, that he never would be, that he was not going to work with animals any more when he is a man. But one thing he will do. He will go back to Holland."

"Back to Holland!" Libby echoed, her eyes widening. It shocked her to think of anyone hating Canada so much that he planned to leave it as soon as he was old enough.

Elsje nodded.

"My father likes Canada, but Piet does not listen, and Father is growing unhappy because Piet is so unhappy. I am afraid that, if Piet does not get better soon, my father will take us back."

The three girls sat in silence. Sal's thoughts were whirling about in a mad scramble. Piet was like her after all—not crippled, but wanting to go back. How terribly she, too, had wanted to go back. Dad had tried to talk to her, just as Mr. Jansen was trying to talk to Piet, but it had made no difference. Why, all he needs, she thought, is a friend . . . Then she remembered Piet's face, angry and bitter, shutting people out.

"Now Piet has said something new." Elsje was speaking very slowly. "He has said he is like you, Sal. You heard him last night. He said he was *kreupel,* or crippled, like you, and because of you being crippled, you could never train Susie. So I thought . . . if you could, if you could train Susie and show him, he'd have to see that he can do things too. When *we* tell him, he can just say we don't know. He says I can do all the things the other girls can so it is easy for me to say 'Go out and play with the other boys.' But he couldn't say that to you!"

Sal was dumfounded. She stared at Elsje and then shook her head, hopelessly.

"If that is your idea, it's no good," she mumbled. "I wish I could, honest I do, Elsje, but I can't. I've tried already. You should have seen . . ."

Shame and disappointment brought such a lump into her throat she could not finish. Then, without warning, Libby turned on her with a one-word question.

"How?" she barked.

"What do you mean 'How'?" Sal stammered, blinking.

"Just what I said. How did you try to train her, stupid?" Libby demanded impatiently, her hair fiery in the afternoon sunlight.

Elsje's eyes brightened with sudden understanding and she leaned forward, waiting eagerly for Sal's answer. All at once, Sal had the feeling the two of them were ganging up on her. Who did they think they were, anyway, asking so many questions? She had told them she couldn't train Susie. She ought to know what she could and couldn't do. She glared at them, but neither of them seemed to notice. They were still waiting for her to tell Libby how.

"Okay, I'll *show* you I CAN'T do it!" she shouted.

She reached out and gripped Susie's collar. Susie, who had come to share the blanket a couple of minutes before, scrambled up, but Sal held fast. Once more, the battle was on. Once more, she fought to make Susie "Sit!" and Susie fought back with every inch of her. She braced her feet on the ground and tugged to get free. She squirmed. She tried to pull her head out of the collar. And Sal, sick inside at having to look so helpless and stupid in front of friends who were still new and very precious, ordered, coaxed and threatened, her voice sharp with tension.

"Come on, Susie, sit. SIT! No, not lie down. Sit. Sit up. Oh, Susie, quit that. Please, sit."

"Let her go," she suddenly heard Libby say. "You're doing it all wrong."

Sal let Susie go and got ready to tear Libby limb from limb.

"Since when do you know so much?" she started hotly.

Elsje interrupted. Her words, soft-spoken, almost shy, fell comfortingly on Sally's sore heart.

"Don't. Please, don't," she said. "Sal, if you could train her, would you like to do it?"

Sal bent her head. Two tears splashed down on her clenched fists.

"I've told you," she got out. "I've already said I'd like to. But I can't, so why don't you both leave me alone!"

"If you really want to," Elsje said, her voice still gentle, but very firm and knowing, "I think you can do it. Wait till I finish. We could get a book. I know there are books and I remember things Piet used to do. I know you could not do it without help. My idea is that we would do it together. I would bring Willem and Libby will bring that dog she has, that fat one, Chum . . ."

"Chum!" Libby squeaked, all her self-assurance gone in an instant. "Oh, no, Elsje, you can't mean that. He doesn't know a thing."

Then something in Elsje's look checked her, for she gave in without putting up a fight. "Okay, okay, I'll bring him and I'll even get some books from the library."

She leaned sideways so that her shoulder nudged Sally's. "Come on, Sal. We're licked. Face it."

Sal held out for a second longer, but underneath she knew she was beaten. She straightened her cramped muscles and gave the other two girls a watery grin.

"It won't work," she warned them, "but I'll try it—for Piet's sake!"

18

Pooch Academy

SAL HAD THERAPY on Friday after school so they planned to start training their dogs on Saturday morning. Sal had a wild hope that the whole thing would be forgotten by then, but when school began after lunch on Friday, Libby slid into her seat at the very last moment holding up some books she had borrowed from the library during the noon hour.

At afternoon recess, the three girls bent over one of them. It sounded simple enough but Sal didn't believe that doing it would be as easy as reading about it. Even so, excitement stirred inside her as she eyed the pictures. Piet would certainly have to eat his words if she could make Susie behave like that!

"Hey, what are you looking at?"

Randy Chisholm had come up behind them so quietly that none of them had guessed he was there. Elsje reached to close the book but it was too late. He had seen. His face lit up and he put out his hand to hold down the page.

"Are you showing them how you trained your dog, Elsje?" he asked eagerly. "I've seen you with him and I've been going to ask you about it. My father gave me a pup for my birthday last year and he's real cute but he's always in trouble. He won't come when he's called, though he knows his name all right. His name's Butch. Would you help me teach him how to behave—the way yours does?"

"I did not train Willem," Elsje explained. She lowered her voice slightly, as she always did when she talked about Pieter, as though she thought he would hear her and be angry. "He is my brother's dog. I do not know how to train dogs."

"Why have you got the books then?" Randy asked suspiciously.

Elsje faced up to him squarely.

"I tell you I do not know how to train . . ." she began again, but Libby interrupted.

"Elsje, why don't you tell him? Randy wouldn't tell and we really ought to have more than three. Willem doesn't really count anyway. If we're going to do it right, we ought to have at least one more."

Sal gasped. It had been bad enough before when she had promised to try to train Susie in front of the two girls. But Randy! Libby couldn't really mean that he should join in their secret plan! Anyway, Elsje wouldn't . . . ! One look at Elsje and Sal knew she had lost again. Elsje had that look on her face, that look that meant she was thinking what would be best for Piet, and when she decided, she would be stubborn as a mule. Now she was studying Randy frankly with her gray eyes and nodding her head slowly.

"You are right, Libby," she said. "It would be good, but it must stay a secret."

"Heck, go ahead and spill it," Randy told her. "I can keep a secret."

The bell rang. Hastily, Elsje and Randy arranged to meet after school so that she could tell him all about it.

Sal waited until the next morning at breakfast to tell the family. Of course, they teased.

"So you're going to jump through hoops and swallow swords, are you, Susie?" Dad asked her, grinning.

Meg looked Susie over thoughtfully and, at last, announced, "She's not long enough to swallow a whole sword, Sal."

"Don't look so worried, Tag-along," Kent reassured her. "They'll let her use a toy sword."

Sal laughed too. The only trouble was, now that she had told them, she knew it was really going to happen. No miracle would suddenly get her out of it. That very morning, Libby and Randy and Elsje—and Chum and Butch and Willem—would stand in her yard watching while she and Susie made fools of themselves.

The girls arrived first. Chum was even fatter than Libby had said he would be. Susie was torn between welcome for Willem and a vast suspicion toward Chum and she wagged and growled at the same time.

Then Randy marched up the walk—and at his heels came Jon Nordway. Randy was carrying a Boston Bull terrier and Jon had a funny-looking pup, with turned-down brown ears and what looked like a black eye, in his arms. Randy's face was very red indeed.

"I didn't tell, honest I didn't," he declared. "It happened with Jon just like it happened with you and me. I found an old dog book we had in the house and I was reading the part on training dogs and he came in and caught me; and right away he said, 'Is that what you were talking to Elsje about yesterday?' Well, what could I say? I couldn't lie, could I? He wants to train his dog, too, and I didn't think you'd mind, once you thought about it. I really, truly won't tell anyone else."

The three girls looked at each other doubtfully and then

turned to look at Jon. Every one of them liked him. Even Sal remembered how he had smiled at her when he had picked up her pencil. He was a quiet boy, but he had good ideas and he did things well. Now, as he waited for them to make up their minds, he glanced down at the funny-looking dog he was holding.

"Her name is Betty Crocker," he offered. "I call her Betts for short."

"Why Betty Crocker?" Libby asked blankly.

"Because she's a mix," Jon answered, his shy smile broadening into a relaxed grin as the other four burst out laughing.

"We need space," Elsje said, getting down to business, as was Elsje's way. "Let's go out in the back yard."

As the group trudged around the house, the dogs lunged at each other. Susie rumbled fiercely. Betts barked sharply, as though she were asking the other dogs' names. Chum waddled along, sniffing at the ground to see if he liked whoever lived here. Butch, the Boston Bull terrier, danced back and forth on the end of a leash, his bandy legs skittering excitedly, his saucy face turning this way and that, not missing a thing. Only Willem behaved properly, walking at Elsje's heel without a single wiggle or sniff to show how interested he was in his classmates.

The moment they reached the back yard, three voices were raised at once.

"Well, first . . ." Libby said.

"Now, we have to . . ." Elsje started.

"I read that . . ." Randy put in.

All three of them stopped and looked around in confusion, each waiting for one of the others to begin again.

Jon, who had not spoken, said firmly, "The first thing we

must do is pick one person to be the teacher. Otherwise, we'll get all mixed up. Elsje's the best one. The rest of us may know what books say, but she watched Piet train Willem and also, with Willem so well trained, she has time to help the rest of us."

Everyone agreed. Elsje didn't waste time arguing. She stepped out in front of them and Sal noticed that her chin had gone up a notch and that she had a determined light in her eyes.

"You must get in a circle, each one with his dog. Sal, stay still. The rest of you, move out. Make it bigger. Leave room between."

The children spread out, hauling their pets behind them. Chum and Betts tangled for a minute and showed signs of starting a war but Libby and Jon parted them and took their places on opposite sides. Sal, with Susie straining on the leash, felt her balance wobbling dangerously. She hoped desperately that whatever Elsje wanted them to do first would be easy.

Elsje ran her glance around the circle, checking positions. Then she made a short speech.

"The first things we will work on will be 'Heel' and 'Sit.' When you say 'Heel!' your dog must walk behind your left heel, as Willem does." She showed them how Willem did it. The moment she stood still, Willem sat neatly. "Then you have to teach them that when they are at heel and you stop, they have to sit until you are ready to walk on. We will start with you all walking around the circle keeping your dog at heel. You must only give one command at a time—and always use the same words. Say your dog's name each time—'Chum, heel!'—like that. Hold the leash not too tight. Do not drag him. Let him follow you by his own self, but when he starts to go away from you, jerk him back *hard* and say 'Chum, heel!' again."

Elsje looked at them and they looked back, their faces serious. Sal shifted her weight, trying to hold firm in spite of Susie pulling away from her. How was she ever going to . . .

"I will do it with Susie so that you can see what I mean," Elsje said.

She came and took Susie's leash from Sal's hand. Sal gaped at her, the way somebody who was drowning would gape at her rescuer. Elsje grinned.

"You walk Willem so you will get used to giving the orders. I have been working with him and I think he now understands English," she said. Then she looked down at the little white dog. "I will do it differently with Susie. I do not see how she could walk beside you with your crutches there. Already I have seen that she walks right behind you most of the time, so we will try to teach her to do it that way."

Elsje turned to the rest of the group.

"Watch," she said.

She leaned over, put a firm hand on Susie's rump and shoved her into a sitting position while she said briskly, "Susie, sit." Susie looked so startled they all laughed. "Do that every time you stand still," Elsje told them, "and make sure they stay down. Don't forget to praise them, either." She gave Susie a pat.

"All right. GO!"

At once a chorus of voices said all at the same minute:

"Chum . . . Susie . . . Willem . . . Butch . . . Betts . . . HEEL!"

The circle began to move. Sal, with Willem trotting obediently just behind her left crutch, watched Susie anxiously. She followed along behind Elsje for a moment but then lost interest, and turned to look for Sally. Right away, and in no uncertain manner, Elsje yanked her back into place, ordering her sharply, "Susie, heel!"

Sal was suddenly and wholeheartedly furious. But before she could do anything about it, Elsje said, "Stop!" The order "Sit!" sounded in five voices, except that in Sal's case it was needless, for Willem had promptly seated himself the instant she stopped moving.

Elsje bent over Susie so that her voice reached them a little muffled. "Now, while he is obeying you, tell him how good a dog he is." She scratched Susie tenderly behind her ears. "Good girl, Susie," she said admiringly. "Wonderful girl!"

Susie's tail thumped once, uncertainly, and she licked Elsje's wrist.

Elsje straightened up and began to lecture. Although she had seemed to be busy with Susie, she had somehow managed to watch everyone else too.

"Libby, you must not let Chum get so far behind you. And don't slow yourself down for him. Walking faster will be good for him. Randy, when Butch goes off to one side, pull him back quick and hard. When they do something bad, you must make them think it is very bad and you are really angry with them. Never, never make it as though you must say 'Please do this for me.' Make them know they *must* do it, and, when they do it right, they are very clever and good. Jon, Betts is lying down. Tell her she is bad, and make her sit again. She is good at heel."

They worked on for almost ten minutes. By the end of even

so short a time, all the dogs and their owners were breathless and tired, but already the children were sure they could see some improvement.

"Now a rest," the teacher ordered. "Let us give our dogs a chance to make friends."

They gathered at the back step. Sal sat herself down, grateful for the railing which she could hold on to. The dogs began to circle each other and sniff. Libby opened one of the dog books and read aloud. They were following its advice almost exactly. It said to keep the training periods short and to make certain you worked with your dog every day, rather than to keep trying too long at any one time. They decided to meet as a group every Saturday and every Tuesday afternoon after school. Now that they knew what to do, they could each work at home by themselves on the days in between.

Then Elsje got to her feet and looked down on the rest of them still sprawling comfortably on the step and the nearby grass.

"Come on," she said, sounding like Miss Jonas, "we have five minutes more work to do."

The dogs were rounded up. The children got back in their circle.

Then Sal's stomach lurched as she heard Elsje say calmly, "You will try it with Susie this time."

"But I CAN'T!" Sal was about to shriek when Elsje went on. She had every detail planned.

"I will come beside you. That way, I can help by holding on to you when you have to pull her back to you. When we stop, we will always stop by the railing. Then, you can hold it when you lean down to make her sit."

Sal nodded dumbly. She was beginning to see that, though

Elsje was going to help them all with their dogs, it was only she, Sally, who really counted, who had to succeed, no matter what. She thought of Piet and of how Elsje's voice sounded when she talked about him. A sudden picture of his face as it had been in the middle of their quarrel rose in her mind. Shrinking from the memory, Sal saw Elsje's real face before her, the sober gray eyes filled with purpose, the young mouth set firmly, refusing to give in.

In that instant, Sal found a new fear. Gone was her worry about how foolish she would look trying to train Susie in front of these children. Instead, she was filled with dread of failing Elsje and the brother Elsje loved but could find no way to help. Sal shivered. Then she looked at Elsje and took courage. This friend of hers was determined and sure. She would not allow her to fail.

Together they walked Susie at heel. It was one of the hardest things Sal had ever done. She felt as though she had four crutches to hold on to and at least three dogs at the end of the leash. It was, however, much easier teaching the little dog to sit. Sal had to get her crutch out of the way and turn halfway around before she could reach Susie, but, holding the railing, she did it without help. When Elsje stood back and let her manage it alone, Sal was suddenly very glad that she had agreed to try this experiment "for Piet's sake."

When Elsje dismissed the "Pooch Academy," as Randy had christened it, Sal found that she was very tired. She slumped against the house, wishing somebody would carry her in and put her to bed. The others felt the same way. Libby sank to the step "for a little rest," Randy yawned widely. Jon swayed back and forth, a glazed look in his eyes. Only Elsje looked alert and as wide awake as ever.

"Out of the way, Libby," Mother said.

They shook themselves and came alive. Trust Mother to know just the right thing, Sal thought proudly, looking at the big tray laden with cookies and mugs of steaming cocoa. Then Mother laughed and disappeared into the house again. In a few moments, she was back with another tray. This time, it held five bowls of water. The children hooted with delight as the weary students of Pooch Academy lapped thirstily, each from a private bowl.

19

The Only Way

SAL KICKED the side of Susie's box again.

"You're just a big sissy, as usual," she told herself in a stinging whisper. "Go ON!"

But she stayed on the bed, her foot still swinging in savage jerks, her eyes dark and stormy. It was Sunday afternoon. In fact, Sunday afternoon was halfway over—and she had promised the others to work with Susie every afternoon. If only Kent and Mindy would go out, maybe she could . . . But they would be here other afternoons. It was no use.

"If you're going to do it, you'll have to do it without caring whether they're watching or not," she said, this time speaking right out loud.

"What did you say, Sally?" Meg, coming into the room, stopped and waited for Sal to answer. Her eyes were like a kitten's, big and full of curiosity.

Sal did not answer.

"Sally, I said 'What did you say?' Now you're supposed to tell me what—"

"Scram, Maggie. I said Scram, Maggie! That's what I said."

"You quit calling me Maggie. My name isn't Maggie."

"Maggie!"

"My name's NOT Maggie! You can't call me Maggie."

"How are you going to stop me, Maggie?"

"I'll shoot you!" Meg threatened, her rage mounting to near-frenzy. "I'll kill you with my bare hands! . . ."

"Meg," Mother called, "go back outside. Go on now. Shoo!"

She came to the doorway and shepherded Meg, who was muttering about "bows and arrows," out into the hall. Then she looked at Sally coldly.

"Whatever is bothering you is no excuse for tormenting a four-year-old. Hurry up and snap out of it. You're wasting a beautiful afternoon."

Despair settled over Sal like a thick black cloud. She stopped kicking Susie's box and her head drooped lower and lower. She didn't look up when Melinda came in. There was nothing Mindy could do to help her. In fact, Mindy was the one she dreaded most. The minute she went out there and tried to train Susie and everything started going wrong, as she knew it would without Elsje there, Mindy would begin to say "You can't train a dog. You can't do it." Ever since Sal had come home Mindy had been saying "You can't!"—and mostly she had been right.

"Sal," Mindy said hesitantly to the bent head.

Sal fought to keep from crying. She kept her face hidden and did not answer.

"Sal, I was wondering . . ." Mindy began again—and stopped.

That wasn't like Melinda, stopping in the middle. Sal looked up.

"Wondering what?" she prompted sharply.

Mindy fiddled with her belt buckle. She shuffled her feet. Sal stared at this gawky, speechless girl and could not believe her eyes. This was never Melinda.

"Aren't you going to train Susie? Well, I mean . . . Didn't you say last night that you were going to work with her every day?"

Sal's eyes bored into Mindy's face.

"Why?" she barked. "What does it matter to you anyway?"

Melinda backed up a step and blushed a deep rose. Sal waited, every inch of her braced, for the words "Because you can't do it yourself, that's why." But Mindy just stood there. Then, all at once, she sat herself down on Meg's bed with a thud and plunged into speech.

"Sal, haven't you noticed anything different about me? Don't keep looking at me like that! I only wanted to help if you wanted me to. I've been trying so hard not to interfere in your life. . . ."

Sal looked into her sister's earnest eyes and guessed the truth.

"Mother's been talking to you, hasn't she?"

"Yes—back when we had that fight about you walking Susie and I said you couldn't. Ever since then," Mindy said, her voice unsteady, "I've been trying not to tell you what I think. Mother said I was trying to live your life for you—and that's what you think I want to do now. But I haven't for ages, and when I said that about Susie, I just thought I might help if I took Elsje's place."

Sal was thinking hard. She had been so taken up with Libby and Elsje that she hadn't noticed before, but now she could see times when the old Mindy would have been telling her what to do or, at least, pointing out what she couldn't do, and this new Mindy had just watched and kept still. Even now, when she was offering to help, she was only asking—not telling. Sal reached out and patted her sister's knee awkwardly.

"Mindy, I'd like. . ." She searched for words. "You never . . . You know, I was just sitting here trying to get up nerve enough to start working with Susie and I didn't see how I could without Elsje."

Melinda sighed with relief and jumped to her feet.

"Come on then," she said. "Here's your crutch. Take hold of the window sill, Sal."

Sal couldn't help groaning inside. Mindy was trying hard and Sal knew she had promised herself as well as Mother that she would go on trying, but just the same Mindy would always be Mindy.

Now she was fastening Susie's leash onto her collar. Leading her, she went ahead of Sal out the back door. Kent, seeing them come out into the sunshine, called down from his tree house:

"Hey, what are you doing?"

"We're going to train Susie," Melinda shouted back. "I'm helping Sal. We don't need you," she added, as he began to hurry down. "I'll try it first, Sally."

Without waiting for an answer, she moved in closer to Susie, placing herself so the little dog was standing at heel. Susie edged away. Melinda moved after her, trying to get their positions correct. All the old anger at her sister boiled up inside Sally. Mindy was not one bit different, not one bit! For once, she, Sally, knew what should be done and for once Mindy was the one who was wrong. This time, she would do the telling.

"Mindy, stop," she ordered.

Melinda turned, but her glance was caught by something behind Sal. She looked so surprised that Sal put off what she had been about to say and turned to look too.

Elsje had just come through the door.

"Hi," she said calmly.

"Gee, I didn't know you were coming," Sal said, relief flooding through her. "Where's Willem?"

"At home with Piet." Then, wasting no words, Elsje spoke to Melinda. "You were doing that wrong," she said. "Anyway, Sal should be training Susie, not you. Why didn't you tell her, Sal?"

"I was just going to," Sal said weakly, wondering if she really would have had the courage to speak to Melinda like that.

Mindy faced them, tossing her head.

"She can't do it, if you want to know," she retorted. "I had to help her."

Then her eyes met Sal's—and she remembered. She had promised never to say "She can't," never to take over and do things for Sal. Her glance fell and she tried to think of some excuse for herself. But, at the same moment, Elsje's face lit up with an eager smile. Impulsively, she stepped forward, one hand out toward Mindy.

"But if you want to help, you can!" she cried. "Sal can do it, but she does need help. I came over to help her today, but I won't be able to always. It would be perfect if you would learn how to in the right way, because you are always here. Say that you will! It is just that you must help Sal to do it, instead of doing it for her. It must be Sal who trains Susie."

She stopped just short of mentioning Piet. Mindy, torn between shame at having failed to be the kind of sister she had sworn to be and anger at Elsje for having come just in time to see her fail, still couldn't help catching some of Elsje's excitement.

What really won her over, though, was Sal's "Please, Mindy!"

"Okay," she answered gruffly. "What do I do?"

They spent the rest of the afternoon working with Susie and clustered on the step studying one of Libby's books. A cold wind rose and prowled the yard as they practiced. By the time they were finished, they were all shivering, in spite of their warm jackets. Mindy glanced up at the gray clouds that had now blown overhead and prophesied, "We're going to have some snow soon."

"What'll we do then?" Elsje said. "Where will the Academy meet?"

Sal gave her a loving look.

"Don't worry," she said, confidently, "you'll think of something."

Elsje failed to smile. She stared back at Sally for an instant. Then, in spite of the fact that she had her coat on and was ready to go, she said, "Let's go in your room for a minute. I must talk to you "

Mindy had gone off to set the table for Mother, so it was easy to slip away unnoticed. Wondering, Sal followed her friend. The instant the door shut behind them, Elsje turned to her, her eyes dark with anxiety.

"Oh, Sally, we have *got* to get Susie trained," she cried in a low voice. "Piet . . . Today I went to take him his clean clothes and he was lying on the bed and he was crying."

"Crying!" Sal echoed blankly.

"At first," Elsje went on, "he would not speak to me even.

but then he said he was so unhappy, that he wanted so much to work with Willem and other animals again, but he knew he could not do it. And he just kept on saying he could not, he could not, he could not, no matter what I said. It was terrible. I didn't know what to say, Sal, except that I was sure he could. He said he was so lonely here, but when I tried to say I was so sorry, he got angry and hard again, like he is all the time now. He said to get out of his room so I had to go, but Willem would not leave him, though he told him to go too. When I came here, they were in there together with the door shut."

"Gee," Sal breathed, her eyes round with horror, "what will we do?"

Elsje stood without answering for a moment. Then she squared her young shoulders. Her words, when they came, had a desperate ring to them.

"We'll just have to go on with Susie. I can't think of anything else. I've tried and tried, but I cannot think of anything else at all."

20

Disaster

A WEEK had passed and Pooch Academy was firmly established when the first snow came. It shook down from the sky like a huge cloud of soapflakes and smothered Riverside in white. The Copelands, waking up and seeing a new world through their windows, collected at the back door to watch Susie's reactions.

"Her first snow," Meg said solemnly. "Her first snow, isn't it, Mummy?"

"The first she'll remember, at any rate," Mother said, smiling.

Meg looked worried for a moment, as she waited for Sal to get the door open.

"It's not my first snow," Meg said stoutly, and then she saw it and smelled its wonderful, cold, damp, Christmas-y smell, and she capered around on the step, getting her bedroom slippers soaked, shouting:

"I remember! I remember the snow!"

Susie loved it too. She kept shoving her nose deep into the fluffy whiteness, only to jerk it out again and sneeze mightily. She tore around and around the yard, almost disappearing where the snow had drifted to the depth of nearly a foot against the fence. She rolled in it and chewed it and, as Kent said, put on a "one-dog Snow Circus."

Seeing the ordinary brown and bare world changed into a

shining fairyland thrilled Sal, but when it was time to leave for school, it was impossible for her to cover even the short block and a half on her own. She stood stock still in the middle of the front walk, not daring to move lest her crutches slide right out from under her, and she thought: How awful—not to be able to go to school! A month ago, she would have been overjoyed. Now she could not bear to miss even one day.

"Waiting for your chariot, I see," Dad said, right behind her.

She thought he was teasing, but she should have known that he and Mother would have thought ahead to this day. Since they lived so close to the school, Mindy and Kent were going to take turns pulling her on a sled when the snow was deep enough, and on other days, when it was slushy or there was a blizzard, Dad would drive her there on his way to work. With much laughter, Dad loaded Sal, her books and her crutches onto the sled. As he tucked her coat up so it wouldn't drag and get under the runner, Susie growled fiercely at him. Kent grabbed the rope and pretended to pull.

"I can't budge her," he puffed. "Dad, I just can't do it for less than five dollars each way!"

Elsje and Libby, late because of having to look all over the Reeves house for Libby's snow boots, came running up and exclaimed over the sled. Then, with a great deal of shouting back and forth, they set off.

Once, not so long ago, Sal would have dreaded jolting along in a sled, the center of a crowd of noisy children, but now she came to love the days when she flew down the walk behind Kent or Mindy, Libby or Elsje, holding on to her crutches for dear life and doing her best to keep the whole sled from toppling over into a drift. Snowballs sang about her ears.

Smaller children hitched rides, standing up behind her for a couple of seconds before they were yanked or ordered off. Other girls and boys borrowed her crutches and swung along the snowy sidewalk, landing squarely on both rubber boots between each swing. It looked so easy when they did it, Sal thought wistfully, but even they, sometimes, put one crutch down on a bit of ice so it went skidding out from under them.

From the moment Sally first saw the snow, another worry beset her. Where would the Pooch Academy meet? She had grown really interested in training Susie, in spite of Susie's discouraging slowness to learn anything. She could, of course, go right on working with her in the house. There was enough room in the hall. But it added so much fun to it all, working with the others, and comparing your progress with theirs.

Jon was doing the best job. On Saturday, Betts had been able to heel perfectly and had forgotten to sit only three times. Most of the time, Jon didn't even have to give the order "Betts, sit!" any longer. Now they had all started to work on "Sit! Stay!" and, although Sal tried not to let the others see her excitement in case she was wrong, she had noticed that Susie had seemed to understand what she wanted right from the beginning. Sal would motion to Susie to stay, and would say "Susie, stay," and then Sal would walk several steps away from her. If Susie started to follow her, she would say sharply, "No, Susie, STAY!" And Susie would! Every time they tried it, Sal had to laugh; for even while she obeyed, Susie always looked so terribly worried, as though she thought Sal might easily leave her sitting there forever. Next, Elsje said they would teach the dogs to come when called.

What if they could not meet together any longer?

Libby came up with the perfect solution. Her family had a two-car garage—built by the last people to live in the house—and no cars! Her father was happy to let the children use the space. The Pooch Academy moved in and Sal liked it there better than she had in her own back yard. The concrete floor was easier to navigate on than the bumpy lawn had been. Besides, the garages were special in a way of their own: bare and empty, with echoes coming from their dark corners. Now, when the Academy members met, there were often six, for Melinda stuck with it, helping Sal the way Elsje had wanted her to and finally getting just as interested as the rest of them.

Sal had never been so busy. What with going to school and having therapy and training Susie and just being part of the family, she had hardly a spare minute. Once in a while, especially when she was in bed at night, she thought back to the way she had felt in those first days after she had come home to stay. It was like her favorite books where everything goes wrong and then turns around and comes right in the end. Somehow, she was sure it would be that way for Piet too. They had another whole month to work with Susie before Christmas. In all that time, they would be able to teach her anything!

On the first of December, she woke to find everything melting. The tree branches were bare and brown again. The eaves dripped steadily and when the children hurried out to the car, it had even begun to rain.

"You wait," Kent said darkly, writing his name in the mist on the window. "There won't be any snow for Christmas."

They arrived at school in the nick of time. Not until Sal was safely in her own seat did she look across the aisle and see that Elsje was missing. On slushy, rainy days, Elsje got a ride with Marjory Corona's father. Sal looked at Marjory, who was in her seat near the back of the room; then at Libby. Libby shrugged. She had just arrived too. The bell rang and the class rose for "God Save the Queen." The next thing they knew, Mr. Mackenzie was explaining Elsje's empty chair to the whole class.

"Elsje has caught the measles," he said, sending a meaningful look at Barney James. Barney had just returned from a bout with them and by now, three others were absent. "Unlike some of you, I think Elsje will be sorry to miss school. Perhaps you could think of ways to make her quarantine easier for her. If you have already had measles, you might be able to visit her when she feels better."

Nancy Schultz raised her hand and suggested that the class write letters to all the children who were sick. Everyone supported the plan with enthusiasm. A committee was picked to buy a card for each child.

The four members of Pooch Academy made no suggestions. They were not elected to the committee. At recess, they gathered glumly in a corner of the playground.

"I never thought about it before," Randy said, "but I sure hate to think of any of the rest of us trying to run the Academy. Elsje can manage us all . . . but nobody else could."

"And she counted on us showing Piet. . . . Of course, she'll be well soon," Libby said hopefully.

Jon looked troubled.

"Yes, but not till just before Christmas holidays start. Then there'll be stuff to do at home and it'll be a whole month before we get going again properly. We can go on working by ourselves . . ."

"We've got to do that," Sal declared, her eyes determined. "We can show her how much we care by doing just that. We've got the book and we can . . ."

Her words trailed off. The truth was that every one of them was slowly realizing what Elsje had meant to them—her grin when you succeeded, her snapping you back to attention when you began to daydream, her cleverness with Willem, and her way of making their work with the dogs mean something. Although they could go on with their dog training, it wouldn't be the same without her. Hers was the spirit which brought them all together and gave them a feeling of purpose and triumph. How could they do without her? Not just at the Academy, but all day long, just as a friend, Elsje was special.

"I wish we could think of something to do for her," Libby burst out. "I mean, sure we can go to see her, but lots of the other kids have had measles and they'll go to see her too. Everyone likes her. And they're all writing letters. I remember when I had measles. No matter how many letters you get, it's still a long time to stay in bed and you itch and you feel bad all over and you just wish something wonderful would happen."

The others nodded. Sal nodded too, although she was sure her memories of measles were different from the rest. Barbara Jean Kirkhorn had come back to Allendale with them, after the summer holidays, and within a few days, seventeen little girls were crowded into the Infirmary. Never had Miss Jonas come so close to looking harried! Never had Sally been so horribly homesick, in spite of all the radios playing, the games, and the cheerful, overworked nurses.

The bell rang. Libby leaned forward, her eyes blazing behind her glasses.

"Listen, we've got to think of something," she hissed as other children jostled past the small group, giving them inquisitive stares as they went by. "We're her very best friends and she's still kind of lonely here and she's worked so hard for Piet and all. We've *got* to think of something different to do for her, just from us."

"Okay," they answered, their faces showing that they felt just as she did. "We'll do it."

". . . If it kills us!" Jon promised, crossing his heart dramatically.

21

Randy's Inspiration

SAL WAS WATCHING Randy when the idea struck him. She almost giggled out loud, for he straightened up so suddenly in his chair he looked as though he'd been electrified. His face became one huge beaming smile a second later, and his eyes began to dance with impatience. It was as though he had whispered right across the room "Just wait till after school!" From then on, the morning was a complete loss for all four of them. Libby, usually so quick with the right answer, stumbled over such a simple thing as 3 into 24. Sal fell hopelessly behind in *King of the Wind,* which Mr. Mackenzie was reading aloud to them, because, in spite of the fact that she'd been wishing terribly on Friday that he would read just one more chapter, she couldn't keep her mind on the story. Mr. Mackenzie had to tell Jon twice to go to the library for a science book, and before noon arrived, he was sending quizzical glances from one to the other of the four excited faces. He stopped asking them questions altogether.

But when Randy told them his idea, they only stared at him in bewilderment.

"We can have a Saint Nicholas Feast," he said.

At their blank stares, he sighed and hurried to explain. At his home, they had a housekeeper who had lived in Holland most of her life. She had told him about Dutch Christmas traditions. On December the fifth, Dutch children put their wooden shoes, filled with hay, outside their doors, and while they sleep Saint Nicholas comes on a big white horse and fills the shoes with toys and gifts.

Randy knew that the Jansens now celebrated their Christmas in Canadian fashion. Elsje had told him, just last week, how strange they had felt changing the way they held Christmas, but that, this year, they were more used to it.

The faces of the other three began to light up with understanding.

"Then they wouldn't be doing anything special that night at all," Libby said thoughtfully.

"And if we could get some shoes . . . and put presents in them . . . Oh, Randy," Sal half-sang, "it's a perfect idea!"

"I think so too!" Jon nodded happily. "We could put some hay in, around the edges kind of, and then put them on the step, and ring the bell . . ."

"And hide," Randy said. "We could hide and watch. If we told Mr. and Mrs. Jansen, they could be sure that Elsje answered the bell."

"Mrs. Mackenzie has some big wooden shoes," Libby remembered, growing more and more shining-eyed. "Remember, Rand, when we studied Holland, Mr. Mackenzie brought them."

It was lunchtime and Dad was waiting for Sal, so they scattered, deciding first that they would tell their families and the Mackenzies, but otherwise keep the whole idea a secret. At lunch, Sal was overflowing with the wonder of their plan. The Copelands, one and all, agreed with her.

"What are you going to give her?" Mindy asked.

"We don't know yet," Sal replied. "We're going to put in some funny things we can find around, just little ones; and then we're putting our money all together for one special present—only we can't think what."

"How much have you got?" Dad wanted to know.

"Altogether, six dollars and thirty-seven cents."

"Gee whiz!" Kent was clearly impressed. "You could get her a chemistry set."

"She wouldn't want a chemistry set." Sal quelled him with a scornful look. "But I don't know what she would like."

She thought again, trying to see inside Elsje's mind. She liked working with Willem, but outside of that, Sal just couldn't put her finger on anything she knew of that Elsje especially liked. Always, when they were together, they had talked about school or Susie—just the other day they'd talked for ages, but it was all about how in the world Sal was going to teach Susie to lie down when she had such great trouble teaching her to sit.

"Elsje just likes dogs," Meg said pensively. She sucked on her spoon and made a funny noise. She went on to make a series of funny noises. Mother reached out and removed the spoon.

"Stupid!" Kent told her. "She's got a dog already."

"No, she hasn't," Sal corrected him absently—"not really. Willem's Pieter's dog."

Then, it hit her. A dog! Why not a dog? One all Elsje's own! Why, that would leave Willem so Piet would have to look after him himself. And Elsje would train a puppy so beautifully—and she loved dogs so much!

Her eyes wide with delight, she turned to Dad, but from his grin she knew he was reading her mind.

"A dog, eh?" he said. "Six dollars?"

Sal nodded, speechless with hope.

"Well, I think that could be managed," Dad told her calmly. "Don't you, Emily?"

Mother's smile was a twin of Sally's, wide and excited and shining.

"I think it's a marvelous idea—and if they need a few dollars more, surely we, the parents of the members of the Pooch Academy, could contribute a little to such a worthy cause."

The minute Sal got back to school, she hustled her three friends off to a secret meeting. The thought of giving Elsje a dog appealed to all of them just the way it had to her. They began to figure out what else they could give—a peg game someone had given Jon and his brother when they had measles, a plastic flute of Randy's which Elsje could play in bed, one of Sal's two copies of *Little Women,* a book of paper dolls which Libby never had time to play with ("They might not be bad if you were sick," she explained), a rubber ball of Susie's (she now had three) and a collar which Chum had worn for a little while in his slim youth. It was easy.

"We'll never get it all in the shoes," Libby commented, "but who cares? If it spills over, all the more fun for Elsje!"

After school, they stayed in their seats, much to Mr. Mackenzie's surprise, and when they were sure the last child had gone and Randy had even checked the door for eavesdroppers, they trooped up to his desk and poured out the whole story. With four people telling it, it got slightly jumbled. Halloween was mentioned, Willem, Sal's secret Place, the Pooch Academy meetings in the garage. The only thing none of them said anything about was how all this was related to Piet. They had all agreed, beforehand, that *that* was a story which belonged only to Elsje.

When they finished, all a bit breathless and excited, their teacher gave them a grin not unlike Randy's.

"Of course we'll donate the shoes," he promised. "The only thing is, I'll want to come along and see the surprise. I've had measles too, you know."

"Sure," Libby said. "It's getting to be really funny, though. Sal's dad and mother are driving us and Randy's and Jon's insist on driving them over. I know right now that, car or no car, my mum and dad want to come too. Half the town will be there before we're done. My big brother thinks it's a terrific idea and he's in Piet's room, so he wants to come, and Jon's brother is his best friend . . ."

They all laughed. Sal wondered where they would ever manage to hide so many people, but she didn't really worry about it. She was positive everything was going to be perfect.

"It's a good thing," Randy said dryly, "that I'm an only child!"

22

So Many Saints

THE WEEK crawled by. There were school and therapy to go to, presents to wrap and plans to make, and a call to pay on Elsje so she wouldn't start wondering what they were doing and suspect anything.

Dad took Sal and Libby and the boys to buy the puppy on Thursday after school, yet even after that time dragged. Sal felt as though she had been waiting forever. Then, all in a minute, it was the Eve of Saint Nicholas.

Sal could hardly eat supper. Every bite choked her. Her stomach was doing cartwheels and she spilled one thing after another. Libby, who was driving over with the Copelands, arrived at the door half an hour ahead of time in exactly the same state.

"It *must* be time!" she said, staring wildly at the clock.

"Sit down and compose yourself, Elizabeth," Mother told her. "The Mackenzies won't be picking up your folks for fifteen minutes yet. We don't want to sit out in front all by ourselves and have Elsje look out and spot us!"

It was dark and very cold outside when they finally started. Sure enough, everybody was going—all four families, plus the Mackenzies!—although everyone, except the four children, had agreed to wait in the cars and just watch from there.

Sal quivered with a mixture of tremendous happiness and almost unbearable suspense as they drew up to the curb in front of the Jansens' house. The puppy whimpered and wriggled on her lap and, with jerking hands, she tried to straighten the red ribbon tied rakishly around his neck.

He was a tiny cocker spaniel, a gleaming honey-color, with the longest, softest ears Sal had ever seen and the biggest, lonesomest eyes. Randy came hurtling across the yard, his boots squeaking in the new, dry snow.

"Come on!" he whispered urgently. "I'm so scared she'll look out and see us."

"Mr. and Mrs. Jansen wouldn't let her," Sal whispered back.

Libby scrambled out first and reached back for the puppy. Then, Sal got her braces locked, Kent gave her a push from behind, and Randy steadied her while she got a good grip on her crutches. Jon loomed out of the darkness to join them and they started for the house.

In the silence, Sal's braces clanked terribly and she prayed: "Dear God, make Elsje deaf or something for just a few minutes."

Then they reached the doorstep; Randy put the two big shoes down without making a sound. Sal looked at them with admiration. They were big enough for a man to wear, and, decorated brightly with paint around the top, they even looked Christmas-y. Jon lined them with a couple of handfuls of hay; and then, Libby knelt and placed the puppy in one of them. A muffled giggle went up from the group. He just fit exactly, but he at once started to climb over the edge.

"Put the end of the string that's around his neck under the shoe to hold him," advised Sal. Libby did so. He could still get out, but this way, when Elsje discovered him, he at least would be beside the shoes. They arranged the other gifts, all brightly wrapped and tied with the gayest ribbon. Libby and Sal had composed a poem to Elsje from Saint Nicholas, and they propped this up in front of the shoes. Sal glowed with pride in it. Neither she nor Libby had ever written a poem before.

It's a long way from Holland
When you come on a horse,
(With a steamer for crossing
The ocean, of course).
But my horse and I,
We made it all right,
To wish you, Elsje Jansen,
Merry Saint Nicholas Night!

The last line sounded too long, but it was what they all felt, so nobody minded.

"Now," Randy whispered, putting the puppy back into the shoe one last time, "you go and get hiding, and when you're ready, I'll ring the bell and hide too. I'll go right down there behind that bush, so pick somewhere else."

They crept off. Sal and Libby went around the closest corner of the house and squeezed themselves against the wall. In a minute, the bell jangled and Randy's boots squeaked hastily towards his bush.

Inside the house, they heard Mr. Jansen boom, offhandedly, "Elsje, see who is at the door."

"In my pajamas!" Elsje said, surprised.

"It will just be the paper put there," her father said quickly. "Go on now. Your mother and I are all seated down."

Feet came across the floor. The two girls stopped breathing as the door swung open.

"Why there's nobody here . . ." Elsje began, but then, as she looked down for the newspaper, she squealed, "SAINT NICHOLAS! . . . MOTHER, FATHER, PIET, PIET! . . . Saint Nicholas has come!"

The Jansens crowded into the doorway. Instead of just taking Elsje in, Mr. Jansen called out into the night, "Come, all you Saint Nicholases, come on now! *Moeder* has cooked you a feast! Libby! Sal!"

Blushing and grinning, the amateur saints appeared from

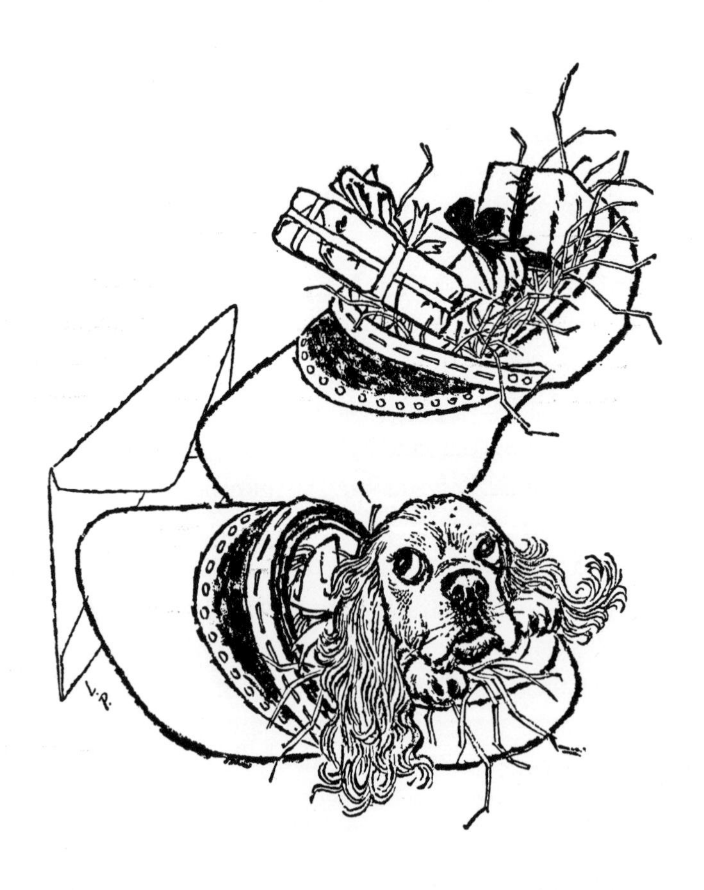

their hiding places. Elsje's face held delight and bewilderment and measles at the same moment.

Mr. Jansen sent Pieter out to the cars to bring in all the families, even the Mackenzies, and within minutes the small living room and dining room were full to bursting with people and dogs.

Then, as everyone gathered around, he lifted Elsje and all her presents to the middle of the dining table.

"Open them, Els," he told her gently as she stared up at him. "They have brought these things all for you."

Elsje did not look at the puppy while she undid the parcels, although he kept getting in the way, clambering over her knees to chew on the ribbons she was trying to undo and getting tangled up in tissue paper. When she had opened all the presents and read the poem, her eyes flooded with sudden dazzling tears. Then, unable to utter a word, she dropped the pile and reached out and scooped up the tiny big-eyed pup. Holding him close, she looked around at the ring of faces.

"Oh," she sobbed, "Oh . . ."

"Never mind, honey," Sal's mother said, her own voice husky. "We understand."

"But I must," Elsje declared, mopping away her tears on her pajama sleeve. "You are such good friends. I . . . Always I wanted . . . I will name him Nicholas—Nicky—after you all!"

There was a round of applause and a great deal of warm laughter. The four Saint Nicks, who had been separated in the rush and now stood wedged here and there in the front of the crowd, beamed at one another blissfully. Then, as Elsje's father moved to lift her down, Mr. Mackenzie asked his question. He meant only to be kind. None of them had warned him. None of them had mentioned Pieter.

"What's this I hear about you running a school for dogs, Elsje?" Mr. Mackenzie asked.

The dogs were all there—shaggy little Susie at Sal's feet, Betts draped over Jon's arm, Chum with Libby's parents, and Butch worrying Randy's trouser-cuff. The teacher took them in with a gesture.

"Can they all do tricks? That's something I'd like to see. How about putting on a show for us?"

He waited, but Elsje did not answer. For a split second, she looked stunned. Then, her eyes grew afraid.

Sal watched her glance fly to Pieter's face. She saw for herself how he tensed as his sister did not speak. An unexpected and unwelcome silence fell over everyone in the room. *Somebody, say something!* Sal wanted to scream.

But nobody knew what to say. Sal was the only one, except for Elsje, who knew the whole story. Even Libby did not know about the day that Piet had cried. Even more important, Sal was the only one who had felt in her own heart the fear that was paralyzing Piet at that moment. Elsje couldn't speak. For once Elsje did not know what to do to save herself or her brother. She could only sit there on the table and stare at him, her face as white and sick as his.

"You're right, Mr. Mackenzie," Sal said loudly enough for everyone in the room to hear. "Elsje has been teaching us how to train our dogs. But really it is Piet who knows how. We can't show you our dogs doing tricks. They're just beginning. It wouldn't be fair to try. But Piet could show you what we *will* be able to do, because we are all doing it just the way he did it first with his dog, Willem."

She gulped, tried hard not to hear a gasp that must have come from Elsje and went bravely on.

"Elsje told us that lots of people thought a young boy like Piet would never be able to train a dog properly, but they all had to take it back. Get Piet to show you right now. Willem is wonderful."

Her courage was gone as suddenly as it had come. She wished she were anywhere but there. She had spoiled everything. If she had kept quiet, they might yet have surprised Piet. Now all Elsje's work was for nothing.

Mr. Mackenzie turned to Pieter. The look he gave him was a quiet challenge. Sal, remembering that first time the teacher had talked with her after school, knew just how it felt to be under that steady gaze.

"How about it, Pieter?" he asked directly. "To be honest, I've wanted to see Willem perform for a long time. I heard about the two of you shortly after you arrived from Holland. Why don't we all back up and make room?"

Everybody began to move back, leaving the center of the room empty. Mr. Reeves and Mr. Chisholm pushed the table to one side, with Elsje still sitting on it, clutching Nicholas.

Sal stood without moving and kept her eyes on Piet. Perhaps, somehow, she could hold him there—but she knew it would not work. For the moment, he was trapped by people, but as soon as a path to the door had cleared, Piet was going to run away.

Then Mr. Mackenzie spoke to him again.

"You won't mind doing this in front of your friends, will you, Pieter? It will make Elsje's Saint Nicholas Feast perfect. Elsje must be a pretty special sister to have."

"You can do it, Piet!" Sally could not help whispering. "You can do it."

He must have heard her. He turned his head and they faced each other for the first time since their quarrel. Mother, Dad, Libby, even Mr. Mackenzie, most of all Elsje, saw the look that passed between them and guessed something of what it meant, but only Sal and Piet really knew how much was said without words when their eyes met and held. It was over in a second. Piet turned back to the man who stood waiting for his answer.

"I will do what you ask," he said, his head high.

He stepped out into the cleared space. Sal held her breath.

"Willem, *volg my.*"

Willem, nearly out of his mind with joy, darted into place at his master's heel. Piet's voice came more clearly and with greater confidence as the little dog obeyed command after command without a mistake. Sally, who had seen Willem do all of these things for Elsje, saw something entirely new as she watched him working with Piet. There was such love between this boy and his dog that they seemed to think together. Often Willem was obeying orders before Piet had finished giving them.

Ralph, Jon's brother, who was very like Jon in his steadiness and insight, applauded loudly at the end, and said impulsively: "Just wait till the class hears about this! I have a dog too, you know, Piet—away better than that mutt of Jon's! We'll start a class of our own and show these kids how!"

Mr. Jansen's voice drowned out any answer Piet might have made as he invited everyone into the kitchen, where food was waiting—rare and wonderful sandwiches and cookies which Mrs. Jansen had had a dreadful time keeping hidden from her daughter. He ushered them all in, beaming, and then swept Elsje, puppy and all, up into his arms and deposited her in a big easy chair in the living room. There she sat for the rest of the evening, having food and drink carried to her as though she were a princess.

Sal, jostled about in the crowd of parents, children and dogs, was suddenly tired right to her toes. The happiness that had burned inside her so fiercely an hour or so before was now turned to a great, quiet joy. Libby got close to her for a minute, but then—"I'm going to get another helping of cake," Libby smiled—and she was gone.

Ralph Nordway and Jimmy Reeves were off in a corner with Piet. Sal peered around people who kept getting in the way. The two Canadian boys seemed to be doing most of the talking, but although Piet still looked tense and stiff with them, she could see him trying hard to find words with which to answer their questions. He was going to be all right. She had not hurt him after all.

Now I can just train Susie because I want to, she thought. She stepped forward, and stumbled. A hand caught and steadied her. She looked up, ready with words of thanks, and found her own mother and father right behind her. Her father gave her elbow a gentle squeeze before he let it go.

"That's my girl," he said softly.

And Sal saw that her mother's eyes were shining with tears.

She turned to face them, managing her crutches clumsily because her arms felt so limp. It had been quite a day. She was going to say something to her parents, but she could not remember what it was. She was suddenly glad that they were there, taking care of her.

"It's time we went home," Dad said. "I'll go tell the Jansens and get Meg. Libby is going with her family and the Mackenzies. I'll meet you in the hall."

"Go ahead, dear, I'll be there in just a minute. I want to tell Elsje's mother how lovely the food was." Mother slipped away.

Sal plodded out into the dimly lit hall. It was good to be there away from the people and the noise. Then, all of a sudden, she was not alone any longer. Elsje had seen her leave and had slipped out after her. She spoke now in a hurried whisper, her gray eyes serious and full of love.

"I just want to say thank you," she said. "I was too afraid to do anything. I would like to give you something, but everything that is here is yours already."

She turned and ran from the hall, leaving Sal staring after her.

What Elsje had said made no sense at all, but maybe it was because she was so tired. Everything seemed muddled right now. Just two months ago, she had been Scarey Sarey. She had been afraid of everything—dogs, people, school, even dressing herself. And now, tonight, here she was with all these people —and she wasn't afraid at all! Only for a moment, for Piet. She had friends, special friends: Libby and Elsje and Randy and Jon, and maybe even Piet now . . . all hers. Was that what Elsje meant—friends?

A wet tongue swiped across her leg and she looked down into Susie's bright knowing eyes, peering up at her through their shaggy thatch.

"Oh, you too, Susie," she murmured softly, joyfully. "You're mine too—mine for keeps!"

And Susie's tail thumped out a decided "Yes" on the Jansens' hall carpet.